T0114435

Praise for Ben Marcus's *Notable American Women*

"Ben Marcus has been accused of redesigning the ordinary sentence, of emptying words of their meaning and injecting them with new, of treating grave matters (such as family and humankind in general) with farcical disrespect, and of blowing away traditional narrative structures with a diabolical wind. And all this may be true. But for those who would describe this work as fantastic, surreal, and anti-real, I can only say this is Ohio exactly as I remember it. Jane Dark was my fourth grade teacher."
—Robert Coover

"*Notable American Women* is an enchanting and moving novel. Like Italo Calvino and Lewis Carroll, Ben Marcus reconfigures the world that we might see ourselves in a cultural and moral landscape that is disturbingly familiar, yet entirely new. [A] wonder book, pleasurable and provocative."
—Maureen Howard

"Ben Marcus's *Notable American Women* is killingly . . . funny, and creepily sad. This book represents an unmediated thrusting toward love with an arsenal of intellectual alienation, and just as forcefully, a thrusting toward alienation with an arsenal of brotherly love."
—C. D. Wright

"Ben Marcus's novel is funny and touching and full of movement and sound, all of which is even more remarkable since the book itself is about stillnesses . . . Marcus investigates—with equal passion—the intricacies of a new mythology alongside the intimacies of a broken family. This is the kind of strange and beautiful book you just want to have around, to dip into again and again."
—Aimee Bender

"*Notable American Women* gives us, with great panache and in eerie detail, a world that is cruelly reasonable within the near-religious limitations of its weird laws and customs. It is a book as unique as it is wonderfully strange."
—Gilbert Sorrentino

Ben Marcus

NOTABLE
AMERICAN WOMEN

Ben Marcus is the author of four books of fiction. *The Age of Wire and String, Notable American Women, The Flame Alphabet,* and *Leaving the Sea* and he is the editor of *The Anchor Book of New American Short Stories.* His stories have appeared in *Harper's, The New Yorker, Granta, The Paris Review, McSweeney's, Tin House,* and *Conjunctions.* Among his awards are the Berlin Prize, a Guggenheim Fellowship, and a Whiting Writers' Award. He lives in New York City with his wife and children.

NOTABLE
AMERICAN WOMEN

a novel

Ben Marcus

VINTAGE CONTEMPORARIES
Vintage Books • A Division of Random House, Inc. • New York

FIRST VINTAGE CONTEMPORARIES EDITION, MARCH 2002

Parts of this book first appeared in *Bomb, Conjunctions, Fence, Harper's,
McSweeney's, Pushcart Prize* volume XXV, and *Tin House*.

The following organizations supported the writing of this book,
and the author is grateful for their assistance:
The Mrs. Giles Whiting Foundation, the National Endowment for the Arts,
the Fund for Poetry, the Art Development Committee,
and the Corporation of Yaddo.

Library of Congress Cataloging-in-Publication Data
Marcus, Ben, 1967–
Notable American women / Ben Marcus.
p. cm.
ISBN 0-375-71378-6
1. Young men—Fiction. 2. Emotions—Fiction. I. Title.
PS3563.A6375 N68 2002
813'.54—dc21   2001045517

Vintage ISBN:978-0-375-713781

Book design by Oksana Kushnir

www.vintagebooks.com

I say an unnumbered new race of hardy and well-defined women are to spread through all these states.
—Walt Whitman

Crying is a weakness of the face.
—Jane Dark

Contents

NOTABLE
AMERICAN WOMEN

I

Bury Your Head

I OFFER THIS MESSAGE UNDER DURESS, hungry, winded, and dizzy, braving a sound storm of words meant to prevent me, I'm sure, from being a Father of Distinction. For the sake of those persons in the world who expect leadership, clarity, and a levelheaded account of the matterful times that my "family"— to hell with all of them—has witnessed, I will not succumb to the easy distractions of language poison, even if it kills the body that I'm wearing, even if I become just another dead man who once felt things keenly and wished only for the world to see inside his heart and mind. There is light enough for one hour of transcription each day, and it is within this time that I have assembled these remarks, having carefully considered the true nature of what I think and feel during my other twenty-three daily hours, allotted to me as darkness by my captors, a group also known as Everyone I Used to Love, Who Would Never Have Survived Without Me.

I am aware that Ben Marcus, the improbable author of this book, but better known as my former son, can pass off or structure my introduction in any way that he chooses: annotate, abridge, or excise my every comment. He will have the final cut of this so-called introduction to his family history, and I'll not know the outcome unless he decides to share with me how he has savaged and defathered me for his own glory. He can obviously revise my identity to his own designs, change my words altogether, or simply discard them in place of statements he wishes I would make. I would put none of these distortions past him and will only caution the careful and fair-minded reader to be ever vigilant against his manipulations, to remember that he is a creature, *if* that, of inordinate bias and resentment, for reasons soon to be disclosed, undoubtedly intimidated by the truth only a father can offer. Considering that I fathered him with the utmost precision, I am sorry that it should be this way. I fully expect even this statement to be omitted, given how it might contradict the heroic role he will no doubt claim for himself, in which case it is only you, Ben, my jailer, who will read this. Please let a father say his part. You have done enough harm already.

A father naturally has much to say on the topic of his son. If he chooses not to meddle it is out of respect, or at least politeness toward this young "man" and his grievous errors. To show too much knowledge of my son's undertaking is to crowd the space the boy must fill in his own time, however slow or errant he might be, however much he lurches into travesty or crushes the father's own deeds with his actions. In such cases, the father, by intruding, obstructs the opportunity for discoveries that mark the basic stages of the boyhood trajectory, in which the son mimes a personhood worthy of the father's own example.

Because the son must learn to behave in a manner in keeping with the father, the father must be a shadow figure at best, a kind of detached bird who can circle and observe without interference, reserving assistance and withholding navigational strategy in order for the son to make a true gain toward the identity of his father, and not cheat into a role that is nearly impossible to attain, that took the father himself many decades to hone and perfect.

Indeed, a father is in no small way the first author of anything the son endeavors to write—is he not?—given the father's cultivation of the little boy, his careful employment of language coaching during that time of youth when the so-called mind of his son was aching to be fed its daily words, and his generous delegation of major family writing tasks—when this country's government hired the Marcus family to study the names of women—assigning the daily written labors to the son instead of hoarding them (as the father might or should have done) to himself. Not to mention an innovative father who allowed an all-vowel language nutrition to be used on his son in order to groom a new and beautiful brain in the boy, a so-called women's brain.

When so viewed, a father can rightly see his own name, Michael Marcus, just above his son's writing, instead of the name of his son. For if his son gathered food and carried it home, that food would become the property of the residing father, to dispense or destroy as he decided, to boil, bake, or bury. So it is with writing that the son might have undertaken and brought to the father for purposes of examination, correction, or criticism. The son is in all effects an *agent of gain* for the father, an employee who happens to share a genetic strategy, a facial style, and posture, though little else, apparently. What the son produces through his labor as a man in this world becomes the property of the father, to consume or discard as he likes, and even the son's name—Benjamin, in this case (or Ben, as it has been diminished in the world at large, a baby sound more fitting to an animal, if that, a word indicating vast and irrevocable disappointments)—can be seen as one of the many stage names adopted by the father, to be borrowed by a person he has set into motion on his own behalf.

It is with sorrow, then, that this father should find such serious fault to Benjamin's "work," if such a generous word might be applied to his writing. I refer, of course, to the book you are holding or that (if you happen to have on hand an orator or nanny who reads you the day's literature) is being recited to you. A father is here inclined to speak critically, and will do so, because of the countless errors and lapses of vision committed by his son, because of the quite un-Marcus-like writing and thinking the son has conducted. How a father wishes that such an intrusion were not necessary and only a quiet celebration were called for instead, an occasion for the Marcus family, such as it feebly remains, to believe once again in its power to exhibit frank statements about the world and its secret histories, a day for such remaining Marcus persons to gather in crew and sip good water together, to breathe in unison and perhaps sing the family ballad, a song I have not heard in some years, as pretty as Family Motivation Music ever was.

Yet such pleasure is not possible, given the travesty of fieldwork on the projects of women submitted here by my son, who is by no means a historian or even a reliable memoirist, entirely lacking in loyalty to the actual world. The very notion at this time of a family reunion is not only suspect but repulsive, and it will not be entertained by any sufficient father, let alone one such as myself, detained in a chamber by his supposed loved ones, surviving despite piped-in language and the occasional presentation of black bread, with strips of "fish" as thin as paper, and vials of highly suspicious behavior water, which I refuse to consume.

Not only are there inexactitudes of an appalling scale in this book, but events, comparisons, and analyses that threaten to fracture a reality that must in every way be preserved, or else forgotten with dignity. Let our lives at least disappear into nowhere, along with everything else that matters. Had my former son undertaken instead a book more in keeping with his abilities—about boats or cars or other craft that boys might need to care about during their period of fascination with motion—a father could be amused by the lovely diversion his son had produced (the world needs more books about the enjoyable objects of our time) and feel no need to offer full-scale rectifications, even if they were required, even had the son scored error after error on the subject, which would have certainly been possible, given his consistent capacity to take what is true and bury it deeper even than his own once-loved father—for his love for me did run at full steam—is buried alive and imprisoned in the field behind his house.

Yet, when the son's topic has so trespassed on the deeds and designs of his former father and the corps of persons once commanded beneath him—to treat, for example, the moments of his demised sister, the implementation of a women's television device to produce new strains of behavior in his person, a secret history of women in the American townships, a supplementary women's chronology of lost events, the vital teachings of the figure known as the Female Jesus, the advent of a women's currency devised by my "wife" to allow an exclusive economy to occur between women, and the ultimate so-called capture of the father by the *person* Jane Dark, together with her listeners and Silentists (I can still hear them shushing me)—the father feels deliberately antagonized and forced into a category of fatherhood heretofore vastly underutilized, that of the Refuser (a word which also means to process and eliminate garbage), who is meant at all costs first to enact a deep and lasting condemnation of the offender, in this case the figure posing as my ostensible son, and next to retract the manuscript, *and all copies,* to its likely destination, the incinerator, where the language upon it might be burned from the page and forever prevented from such a heinous arrangement again. Indeed, I herewith ask all readers, once they have absorbed and studied my remarks, and then transcribed them as an exemplary caution against the treason of children, to forgo whatever follows in this book, all of it certainly folly, I assure you, and burn the thing to cinders with the greatest haste. Bring a hard fire upon it, please, and see it all as an aberration prosecuted by a disease called "Ben Marcus."

Any other father would agree that corrections in this life must always be sought. A son's goal, if the son is operating at capacity, must be to extend the bodily range and mental power of his father, particularly, especially, if that father is interred in an underground compartment where language—I should not need to repeat it—is funneling down in an ever-menacing stream by a man hired to burst the father's body with words. When that task is compromised, the father is expected to speak loudly and with force to ensure that a correction is registered.

The task of being right is a task the father perfects over time. He rehearses various forms of error and attempts at every turn to incorporate them into his arsenal of actions, using the *Behavior Bible* if he must, seeking always to dilate the range of conduct available to a father *and the persons he commands,* remembering that morality (that is, what to do when another animal gets too close) is often regulated by figures unwilling to commit the necessary harms, the incidental bloodshed and trespasses that a mastery of daily life requires, never feeling sure that an act is wrong until it feels *life-threatening* to the father, which can only be signaled by the appearance of the father's blood, or by levels of pain in the father that are unbearable, at which point a powerful verbal gesture—written, spoken, carved into the wall—is required to bring the matter to its correction. Even a muffled voice of a father, *as if uttered from underground,* for fuck's sake, has more force than a clear and booming voice of the boy who is his son. The boy's voice is anyway sheer ventriloquism on the part of the father, is it not, since I cocreated the awful lad? Yet sometimes that ventriloquism, if too accurate, must be adjusted in pitch and brought to a falser modulation, lest an audience mistake the dummy for an actual person with its own heart and head and hands, a boy rather like the father in matters of hair and skin, certainly, but deeply different at the level of mind, only an apprentice—and here a poor one, a stick figure, convincing only if viewed at a distance—to the range of thought the father himself has cultivated.

It should never be forgotten that Benjamin Marcus is being commanded at this and all moments by the person whose words you are reading.

The corrections I mention are not only required to assert

dominion of the father, which here hardly needs doing—since even in prison I can choreograph realistic situations in the living world—but to protect my former son from the wake of disaster inevitably impending when such a degree of falsity and incompetence has been registered, as with the book at hand. He will not be forgiven his mistakes.

Given Ben's statement, however, that the father only possesses a reproduction of what the son has written, indicating the presence of other copies out of the father's range, in areas the father's body is restricted from, the father must here be content with producing a disclaimer that will sufficiently mute *all that follows* of the son's labor, a short introduction to the man acting as my son that might warn a careful reader— because you had better be careful—sufficiently clear of his despicable person.

While Benjamin is not entirely *retarded* in the conventional sense, a slowness and singularity to his behavior have been unfortunately observed, and other fathers and mothers might grimly relate to the lowering of standards that becomes necessary during such situations when the boy in an American family proves to be just slightly craftier than an imbecile. Yes, he can eat and laugh, play simple outdoor games, dress himself in the appropriate gear, and carry on a sensible conversation. Yet one is so eager to witness a son whose mind can operate at the highest levels, who can synthesize the confusion of a world clogged indiscriminately with trees, persons, and repetitive shelters into a regulated drama with causation, revelation, and redemption; a boy who can cut through the mystery of daily life with confidence and thus come to control the people in his range of sight and beyond, simply by outsmarting and outfighting the motherfuckers; yet in the case with the Benjamin figure, the apparition so similar to my son, no such control has in any way been evident. His complicity with mediocrity has been impressively well realized.

Nor do I mean to suggest that a retarded or simple man such as Ben can have no use in a society. I am in favor of a caste system in which the dull, the boring, the slow and sugar-minded American animals—often mistaken for "people" and likewise privileged—are given challenging tasks and rewarded with carefully controlled sexual intercourse, excellent bread and butter, and weekend meat. Ben is a strong lad and can reliably carry sacks of soil, sing a convincing love song, and show unmatched devotion to his "mother." These tasks certainly can find their expression in the world at large without offending or hindering the more necessary living persons. Indeed, the front-runners of civilization *need* helpers such as Ben, and not just for sexual release, but also to fix roads, level trees, and dig position trenches for women's-frequency hijacking.

But if you are in a position to look at this Ben Marcus, who I'm sure will do his best to get in your face at every opportunity and show himself to you (such is his ignorance of his own hellishly depressing appearance), then I invite you to do so, and not uncritically, being honest with yourselves about what you see, and what you don't, allowing your deepest judgments to emerge. It will help to scan smartly away from his form on occasion to the more realistic objects in the landscape—the trees and houses and people that happen to fill your view, or the bookcases, lamps, and flowers—in order to appreciate just how wrongly Ben's body juts out of nothingness into a space worthy of a more substantial creature or household object;

considering all the while, if you are able, what a miracle it is that even routine self-examination on his part—while brushing his teeth or soaping his face before a mirror—has not yet led him to quietly end his own life down at the river, with a rope or gun or razor, and give everyone concerned a needed breather from the exhausting obligation of his existence.

Certainly you would, at the least (if you do not agree that he makes a good candidate for a respectably necessary suicide), have to then agree that he cuts a poor form—he is stooped and bald and sad, his gait is a slouching apology against motion, his pockets are empty, the poor fellow has lost his mother, and I would guess that no pretty creature has handled his penis in months. His body is not exactly the makings of a hero, and I warrant it emits much disagreeable waste.

Naturally, a son who is crippled or ill, weak and sad, or palsied with fear at the thought of life without his father— who may or may not have been *brought to ground* by a group that calls itself the Silentists—incites a degree of sympathy in the father. The father remembers those early moments of the Marcus life project, when Benjamin was just a small measure of flesh called a child—the size of his father's hand, but in no way as interesting to look at—when he labored on palms and knees to ascend the ever-dashing body of his father, who moved through the fields with supremacy. At the time, Benjamin enjoyed seeking information within the father's imposing beard, or his soundproof wig, which certainly must have appeared as a nest of treasures, within which something knowable might be discovered. He sought carriage now and again in a swing set built and anchored to the turf by the father, who stood behind the swing to ensure that it traversed an agreeable arc, containing the disastrous body of the son. Often the father strapped Ben into his seat and sent him "Around the World," over the top bar of the swing, and over again, until Ben was panting fast and crazy in the eyes, a bit wobbly on his feet after he climbed back down to earth, but always sweetly smiling, trusting the man who ruled him even when the sensations of that rulership were not entirely agreeable or were beyond the boy's comprehension.

The young Ben was a collector: flowers, buttons, stones, and any scrap of equipment that littered the compound. Everything small that he could remove from the world and bring to his parents' attention. He carried his stuff in wagons and could thrill himself with the littlest achievements, often fancying himself a key figure in the important job of shuttling junk from here to there. It was a sobering but necessary task each time to remind the little fellow that he had not invented these special things—the buttons and stones and sticks, the disposable hearing cups and seared swatches of cotton—that all the world's beauty existed before him, and did not require him for survival. He was just a person, and everything he thought and did had already been thought and done. Perhaps he should seek to discover something that wasn't so obvious and abundant in nature, it was suggested. To say something new, to do something startling. That he has not proved himself capable of even a single original act, discovery, or statement is nearly as damning as his frequent weeping and his neurotically induced deafness.

And while my son's illness, if such it is—the apparent onset of "motion fear" and his supposed deafness to certain words, as spoken by certain people—provides a partial excuse for his failure to come forth as a creature of distinction, a man who might soldier over every difficulty to slaughter his life opponents with great ferocity, either with weapons or through the sheer verbal power that runs deeply in his family (on his father's side), he is, in fact, short of any kind of battle plan, lacks the coordination to even flee from a predator, and is weakly stocked with reproductive fire, given his inability to father very many effective persons during his enforced copulations with the Silent Mothers.

Let it not be said that this father is without an animal response to the son, in which warmth of the old-fashioned kind flows in the chest and a certain pity is forthcoming no matter what feeble *gestures of life* the Ben Marcus system manages to perform, even if the boy were to attempt to physically beat the father, a type of aggression the father is completely prepared for, by the way, no matter how dark it is in here, or how much advantage a creature has who can see his own goddamned hands. The father would beat down the son's attack, naturally, wound him just enough to reaffirm the boy's all-encompassing weakness and widespread failure, and then hold his injured body and attempt a soothing litany of comfort words. I am sure it is what he wants, and it is not beyond me to talk soft. I can make a creature weep and will do it if I see the need, if it leads to a situation I might require within my larger strategy. I have said things to this boy that, if heard by an outsider, would fairly indicate a degree of affection being transmitted. It could easily be understood as love: "There there, little Ben." "Egghead." "Bald Beauty." "Sugar Cheeks." "It's okay, Sweetbread." "Just breathe." "Tiny Shark." "Little Tiny Shark." "Skin Fish." All little nicknames that produce an unreasonable amount of pleasure in his person, cause him to curl up and grin and gaze at the sky.

Oh no, I admit it, the father is truly sympathetic to weakness, frailty, and lost hope in a son, should it be exhibited, particularly when the son has been *regularly tormented in the worst way by an animal,* indeed brought to submission by a dog, and used for unbearable purposes by a group proposing an end to all motion. Allowances are made for every kind of error. Nor is it that a father wishes to make a case, either legal or emotional, against his son (which is not to say that a good case could not be made, because it certainly could), or wishes that his son would stay his hand at attempting to narrate *events he cannot possibly grasp,* whether or not they happened to him, or concepts that, when presented without the appropriate theory and context, such as the Weather Museum, for Christ's sake, the Clay Head of Jesus, and the Women's Frequency of Sound, *appear ridiculous and untrue,* and will be believed by no one, dumb ass. A father is pleased anytime a son can regulate his busily superficial mind for the time required to command a book's worth of language to the page. Such a feat is particularly notable, given the aforementioned mental challenges of the son, when it can barely be expected that the son remember to bring potatoes to the underground area where his father waits to be fed. When his only task is to *bring a potato to his goddamned father,* or to let new air into his father's area, where the old air has already been used, because there is a living man down here!, or to walk his father up above when his father has gone months, motherfucker, without seeing a house, a stick, a bird, a window, a road, *the key objects of our time,* when his father has no new air to clean his eyes and rid his skin of the language fluid poured

in by the man with the tube, who speaks his Sentences of Menace, trying to burst the father's body with words. Let a man
wash himself, and stride in the open air, for fuck's sake! Given
his systematic incompetence and neglect of the one person he
was born to love, how can a single word from Ben Marcus's
rotten, filthy heart be trusted?

Granted, I love my son dearly. He has been a sweet boy at
times (I can picture his long head sailing through the air like a
ball), and rather touching to observe, despite his failures. He is
cute, with his wet red mouth, and it would no doubt be interesting to dress him in a costume to entertain the members of a
picnic, to inflate balloons and dazzle the children, perhaps, or
to pretend he was a horse or some other simpler creature of
this world.

I love what keeps me alive, and my son is an extension of my
body, a prosthesis, you understand, that I can dispatch on my
behalf to prowl my former house, to collect objects, or witness
conditions that might prove to be a revelation upon examination. A father must continually be in a state of study, should he
not? I care for this fellow because he is an apparatus that can
investigate areas my own local body can no longer achieve. In
that sense, my son is the part of myself that still operates *at
large*. And although physical harm to his body does not technically hurt me, if his body were prevented from its task in the
greater world, if he were finally captured by the authorities
(that is, if personal failure and disappointment were policed
and punished by law), my own body would eventually suffer
because its special flesh satellite had been severed. There is also
a small chance that I might starve without him.

You might think that ditto is true for your son, that all of the
above applies in spades to whatever awful creature you fucked

for and birthed into the Ohio pasture to grow into some kind of person who would only live to fail repeatedly before your eyes, to wither, no matter how you watered him. Nothing could be worse than to watch one's own bodily product fail to learn to swim, I'm sure, or smash his teeth on the rung of a ladder and be forever a kind but ugly man.

But you cannot share my grief unless your son is also a shandy, but not the kind of shandy who crouches over men's hips to host the probing of their genitals, but rather one who is supplicated to the dog of the house—you heard me—the quietly elegant creature on all fours who seeks and finds dominion over your son with hygienic regularity, who tracks him down outside in the yard or inside in the den to play horsey, a dog and a man playing horse, giddyap and let's go at it, this creature all over your son, who is too scared, or too secretly pleased, to assert his evolutionary supremacy and beat back the amorous advance, until his shoulders are calloused from the paws of a dog and he practically wears an apron for the animal, so total is his submission.

There is then a point when a father says so long, farewell, good-bye to a boy who has traversed so far from actions that might be considered human that he is only the bitch of a beast who eats out of a bowl, a kind of whore to a four-legged "man" that has him in every room of the house and in the field or at the pond and even on the flannel pillow in the kennel. The father becomes deprived of the child; he enters a state of child minus and is in need of a new brood.

It is therefore asked that those examining this written artifact, or listening to its delivery, defer to the voice of *this* father, the overfather, the father of fathers. If confusion results in such a pursuit—if too many fathers present themselves as figures of authority seeking to exercise power upon your person, to caress or handle you, to dictate the dangers of the day, or to weep just when you doubted their humanity—let it be remembered that the father who commands your attention *at this very moment* should be given dominion over whatever local father happens to obtain in your vicinity, even if that local father appears familiar and kind, the lover of your mother, warm, a dispenser of money, and fatherlike in other comforting ways. Even if he is the man who appears to be posing in those old photographs, holding an early version of you in his arms and possibly kissing your head. If a picture of him now makes your chest come aglow, if speculation or remembrance of his death causes empty black alarm—he is at all costs to be refused, please, dismissed and forgotten. You are to consider him a decoy father sent to test your fealty while your real father waits trapped in a hole, fathering you from afar. This is not solely because I am a superior figure to your local father, or because I could reduce your local father to a mess of apologies and contradictions if I were allowed to occupy the same room as he does, to interrogate or debate him on *the complications, the difficulty, the serious flaw to the life project.* Nor is it because I am greater in physical prowess than your local father, could throw him in a pit or storm-fist his body to sleep, beat him in a footrace or humiliate him at chess, outwit him in any conversation about a machine or the building of a house or the theory and use of every tool in his probably inferior tool chest. Nor indeed is it solely because I could twist your local father's arm up his back, then turn him to face you so you could see his agony as he admits that, no, he doesn't love you and how, if it came down to it, he would save himself, would sacrifice you to whatever threat came along, a dog, an intruder, a flood—you're on your own!—because he doesn't want to die either, this man masquerading as your father, the Halloween version, whom I am more than happy to unmask, the fraud.

And this is where you must ultimately prefer me to any so-called father you may have known before.

Your local father is afraid of everything, is only a baby, a whimpering infant who wants his parents, too, needs to be comforted, soothed, supported, and stroked until he sleeps. His secret is that he wishes it would all go away. You in particular; you are only a horrible responsibility made of flesh. Be gone, too, the world and everything big or little inside it, be forever gone, because it is terribly hard to be him, and no one has any idea how hard it is just to stay alive, to breathe freely, to walk along the road without collapsing in fear and fatigue. To just hide and sleep under a blanket where no one can find him, particularly not you, the creature he created, who now expects his holy everlasting love and will not be gone or ever, ever leave him the hell alone.

I vouchsafe that you will not encounter these problems with me.

You'll note that when a man is rendered to an underground compartment, such as the case with myself, he becomes, among other things, immune to category, beyond a single family, a supervisor of the world he left behind. Such a one is the ideal father. He is a man without weather, upon whom weather cannot act. Do not underestimate this. Not rained upon. Not gusted over, or snowed on, or blown over, or burned by the sun, hidden in fog, lost at sea, killed at work, crushed in a crowd, broken in a fall off a bridge, wounded by the words of his wife, smashed with a hammer, washed away in a flood, or ever struck by sticks flying loose in a storm. Everything that has ever happened above ground has been hellaciously awful. There has been no event under the sun that has not killed people. And none of it can touch him. He is outside of circumstance. He wears a shell of earth on him. He is pure mind. Father mind.

Throughout history, all important Command Centers—where key strategies have been decided and the Lost People of this world have been instructed through the haze—all of these Command Centers have existed underground, below the flow of the projectiles that reduce every other creature under the light into such shivering wrecks in need of protection. If your local father is not at the Command Center, *for I do not see anyone else here with me*—if he is sleeping, or tending the yard, or laughing and splashing in a pool—then I ask you how he can be an effective ruler. Is it not true that he has vacated his throne, and is now simply a boy who would cry like a child as soon as he saw me walking toward him? The minute I approached to take charge of the situation, your so-called father would collapse and fold into my arms with tears of relief and become simply one more of my children—*There there*—making him only a brother to you, an older brother who briefly thought he knew something and could lead the way.

But Father is home now and your older brother can stop pretending.

You must trust me and love me and let me lead you free of sorrow and small thoughts, little ones, because God of God Almighty I'm the father of fathers, who knows and thinks and feels so that you don't have to. And you—if you are listening and at all alive and in need, if it hurts and you are scared, and every day is increasingly an impossible prospect—you are my son, my daughter, my little one, all grown-up, so sweet, so tall, a little bitty thing, aren't you, throbbing and new to the hot sun that spotlights your approach over this earth, a joy to behold, my darling creatures crawling so intently over the soil, homing in on the voice flowing out of the hole and through the sticks and shrubs of Ohio and America into your hearts. A river of sound from the mouth of your father. Swim into me and all will be well.

You have always known that I am him, the one to father you home.

Let it happen. Say good-bye to the old. Forget Ben Marcus and his world of lies. I am not the father of such a one, but I am yours, and yours, and yours. Come to me. We're family. *There there.* All will forever be all right.

Your father,
Michael Marcus

2

The Ohio Heartless

———◆———

Shushing the Father

Blueprint

Better Reading Through Food

Dates

The Name Machine

Shushing the Father

I DO NOT RECALL THAT Pal ever resorted to words. Mostly, he just ran and jumped and ate the brown behavior cakes, much like I did, but better and harder. When Pal swam in the learning pond, he dog-paddled with his head up and his tongue hanging from his mouth, as though he had shouted up a thick, dark syrup that froze between his lips.

Pal was a black friend and he growled deeper than an animal. When I growled like him, we made a booming forest sound, enough to bother the women into throwing their listening cloth at us. His hair was one length all over his body, clusters of fine needles on my skin that set me shivering and needing to pee. I had to run to the shrubs and squeeze at myself in private until the terrible itchiness was gone. I wanted to tear him apart to see what exactly he made me feel—to put pieces of him on a table and understand his insides. His hard black head was mostly all I ever saw, a spot of nothing that I wanted to follow. Whatever I couldn't grab and hold and keep was Pal. He was the only thing that wasn't mine, which made me as angry at him as if he were my brother.

I first met him in the arms of the great Jane Dark, who appeared at our house, to a black-carpet reception, along with her army of listening assistants: full-sized girls with stethoscopes and notebooks, wearing streamlined beige hearing suits. The girls stood outside our house that day and looked at our street in grim fascination, as though they had read somewhere it would soon be destroyed. From my window, I watched them, and they never flinched. Our big fake white house could hardly withstand so much staring; it did nothing but die in place as they stood there. Each girl looked almost the same. Sharp hair in a chunk of bang just over her eyes, a body buried under cloth, white shoes shining against the soil like spilled paint. An embarrassing amount of sunlight glowed on the cups the girls all held in their white-gloved hands. It was enough to blind someone who might be trying to figure out who they were.

Later into Dark's residency, the girls performed fine outdoor spectacles that reminded us how little we had done in our yard. You see someone using your own house better than you've ever used it, and you go to your room and close the door. Sometimes the girls linked their arms in a human chain on the lawn while Dark worked her behavior removals inside, rendering my mother a perfectly quiet American citizen, teaching her the new silence. The girls would form a line and slice through the air like the arm of a carnival ride. A heavyset young lady anchored the unit, while an eggy little handful of a girl flew in the windy end position. If she lifted high enough on the swinging limb of bodies, she twirled her rope and created vocalizations up there in the air, grabbing leaves and singing, often catching scratches about her face from tree branches that didn't much abide her kind of flight. Sometimes she zoomed by my window and I would reach out and try to touch her, like sticking my fingers into a fan. At night, I could hear the hum of bodies whipping through the air as the girls waited outside for instructions from Dark.

Except Dark did not speak at night because the darkness lowered her voice so much, it frightened her women. She slept in a sentry harness outside my mother's bedroom door, her hands dangling like roots, wrapped in the translucent linen that was starting to fill our house, baffling every sound-making thing until nothing more than the smallest whimpers could escape from it. She rested and kept watch. Even sleeping, she muted our house with her long, soft body, a silence that lasted well into the morning.

Ms. Dark came into our house like an animal who owned something. She walked upright and carried a scary cloth. When she approached some of our furniture or pottery— including old bowls my sister had made, which held her private smelling salts—Dark held the cloth to her mouth, swallowing and coughing at once in a gesture of inventory. For each piece of our property, she raised the cloth to her lips and worked her mouth into it, as though it were a radio she could talk to. I tried to hide from her, but her girls set up so many picks and body barriers that she found me at once and the cloth rose again to her mouth—a dirty white linen, like a rag from my father's shed. All I could see of her face were her flat eyes, puddles of oily color in her head. My mother accompanied her, held the hem of her shirt, and whispered a mouth-straining message into Dark's hood that sounded like the end of a sick animal's breath. I felt sorry for my mother, whose neck wrinkled up in back like an old man's face. From behind, she looked like someone else's father. I had not heard her whisper before, and it sounded as though she might be in trouble, wheezing at the high, desperate end of her breath, where words sound like a failing engine. Dark stuffed the cloth between her lips as she listened, and for a moment it sounded as though she were sobbing, because a heaving arose from within the hood, a stuttering intake of breath seizing her shoulders as if she were feeding from her hands. But when the cloth finally revealed her face and she moved once again among our furnishings, Dark's mouth was dry and bloodless, rimmed with a powdery saliva, and she herself seemed as much without feeling as anyone ever had been in our house.

I stood still as the retinue continued to survey the objects of our home. Two girls slid toward me and pinned a small tag to my pajama top. Their fingers were buttery on my neck and their hair scratched at me like wire. The tag was fastened just under my chin, and I had to scrunch up to see the long code embedded on it, a set of numbers and letters spelling nothing I had read before. I touched the symbols, and they made more sense under my fingers, but before I could figure out a message, my hand was slapped away. Dark lowered her arms as she passed me, and for a second I could smell the cloth go by my face.

The reception carried on in this manner for far too long. When Dark arrived at a window, she took slow postures there in the light—reducing herself so much in space that another woman could have been tarped around her—and we were all supposed to wait there as though we were looking at a painting that might suddenly prove interesting. My mother crouched nearby and squinted at Dark. She tried the postures that Dark had struck, but my mother was too tall and she kept losing her balance, giggling loudly as she toppled, exaggerating her embarrassment, upon which Dark was polite enough not to remark. Some of the assistants stood by my mother and braced her from falling over. I had not seen her allow herself to be handled so freely before. People were actually touching my mother. Other girls made writing gestures in their notebooks, their hands dipping and looping into the paper as if they were sewing up someone's body. I did not need to stand like a fragile old lady while people massaged my arms and held me upright, but standing upright at all seemed difficult in that company, as the women around me did everything but that: crouching, lunging, going airless in their bodies as they draped themselves like pelts over our furniture. Standing made me feel too tall, in charge of something. I thought I should issue a command or make a ruling, but I could only look at one thing, at the man they had brought with them, who hadn't hit the floor yet, who was too perfect for me to see, who would not look at me at all.

Pal was carried from room to room that day because Ms. Dark would not let him walk the floors on his own. "A bomb with a heart," she called him. When his heart stopped, he would go off and there would be a sad time of thunder, with thunder so slow that people would collapse and houses would take great fractures in their sides, with people pouring from the seams, running for their lives. Every time she said "thunder," she squinted at me, filtering the word toward me with her eyes until I forgot what it meant. She said "thunder" as if it were my name. She said it so much in the way I would imagine my mother saying it, if my mother talked and this were the only word she was allowed to say, a word that would have to stand for everything she felt, that I wanted to run out of the house and dive deep into the learning pond, until I had reached the cold, dark bottom. The girls around her nodded in agreement. I didn't like how words sounded on her face: frozen bits of her body she was retching up. We had to be very careful, Dark said; we had to keep Pal alive no matter what. His dying would pull the plug on something terrible. She held Pal in front of her, her white shirt blocked by a great spot of black water in the shape of something living. He had legs that were hard and long and made me hungry. I wanted to be held against somebody so that I looked like that: like nothing, like a hole into nowhere, like a piece of sleep. Jane Dark was someone to disappear against. The whole time she carried him, Pal kept his eyes closed, as though a switch had to be flipped for him to wake up and look around. I moved to the stairs and watched, concentrating my whole head at him to see if he would open his eyes, but Pal slept hard against Jane Dark, with a wet mouth. Nothing I could do in that house full of quiet people would wake him up.

I wandered upstairs. All of these old people in my house made it hard for me to breathe. They were too soft. Somebody might break. No one was singing and there were no sandwiches.

In my room, I looked out the window to see where my father might be hiding. A visit from so many people was bound to frighten him off. He would have run to the shed. He would be peeking from behind a tree. Soon we would hear his scared little song.

The day was pale enough to reveal a finality of mountains in the distance, and everything looked as it ever did: shrubs buried softly in a soil as loose as black rice, the learning pond set too low to the ground, birds flying poorly and without purpose, the sun blocked by a cloud the shape of our house. Above the furnace, a sharp string of behavior smoke was breaking up as it floated over the learning pond. A convoy of small blue trucks glowed on our street as if they were see-through—Dark's vehicles parked in neat formation. A flock of birds must have pierced through a small opening in one of them, because a storm of sharp black bits whirled within, the birds as fast and small as bees in a jar.

Below me on the grass in front of the house, a small man was pinned on his back by a circle of girls. My father did not look as disheveled as he should have, considering what it must have taken for the girls to wrestle him down. It would have been just like him to surrender to their grasp too easily, to play along until he was their prisoner, happy to have so many young women minding after him. All he ever wanted was to be an accomplice in his own capture. He must have sat down with pleasure when they set upon him. He must have exaggerated his alarm when they finally pinned him down.

If I held my breath, I could zoom my sight in right up close to his simple face, to a proximity no son should be allowed, and I quickly saw much too much of my father, an amount of his person I didn't think possible, which made me scared and disappointed by him at the same time. He should not be viewable so close-up, I thought. He should not be that dismissible. The more I held my breath, the more I felt I could leave my room through the window and swoop down through the circle of girls right up against my father's red, struggling face, not stopping there, but entering my father at his hard red mouth and plunging directly to the underside of his face, where I could look back out from his head at a ring of girls' faces encircling a cakelike round of sky, and, far beyond that, see the tiny face of a boy framed in glass, watching me as if it were my turn to be alive. I did not much want to be inside my father's face this way, restrained by children, while my son watched me from his window. No matter how hard I tried, I only noticed what was wrong: the clear flag we had raised alongside the spire on the roof, the unfinished shed where my learning was supposed to happen when Mother wasn't home, and then the learning pond itself, which from my father's point of view looked like an unpromising little puddle and nothing more. The water was muddy and slow and dead. A person might float on that water and never change. He might drink it and still remain himself for the rest of his life.

I breathed. I blinked. I turned my head and exhaled in hard, short bursts until I had shaken my father's perspective. My sight was thin and clean and my own again. When I returned to the window, the picture was foggy and my father was just another man brought to ground by an efficient team of girls, so many of them that he didn't have a chance. He wrestled vaguely against them on the grass, but they kept their feet on him and made clapping gestures in front of their chests. Something about the way the girls clapped seemed to gather too many birds into their midst, a cluster of black objects that fell heavily to the grass. The claps were short and hard, not at all like music; more like a code of command. The birds gathered nearby, and some of them fell to their backs and seemed to rest there, their brittle legs twitching each time the girls changed the cadence of their clapping. None of it seemed to have anything to do with my father.

I cranked the window closed and took off my clothes. It was time to hold my breath and practice fainting. There were too many wrong, new things in the day, and I had to drop away into the sweet brown light of a good four-minute faint, enough to make the day's events seem like someone else's life, happening in a smaller and softer house a good distance down the road from here.

Before I could clear a blackout area for myself—roll out the emotion rug, remove all sharp objects within the safety diameter—I heard footsteps coming slow and heavy down the hallway, someone's body drumming at me. I was not used to visitors. This was the sound of someone making an exciting mistake. The steps were exaggerated, heavy and sarcastic, by someone who must have thought that walking itself was a joke, to be parodied if done at all. Thundering toward me now, the little man. I knew that I would not be fainting for some time. This would be a good deal better than that. My door trembled with his approach. I turned and waited, trying my best to relax my face.

There's probably no other way to describe what Pal did than to say that he found me out with his mouth, that he needed to know something, and the answer was somewhere on my person.

He ran upstairs that first day, free of Dark's arms, and he was yelling in some other language as he jumped up on my bed, a planet of fur and squished eyes, speaking his funny one-syllables, barking the names of people I didn't know, as if he were only a dog.

I couldn't understand what he was saying, but I wanted to do something just as impossible, to show him I wasn't content with anything I could actually be capable of doing—walk the ceiling and speak a new language to my friend, or set fire to my own hands and run circles in the room, but my mouth was built only to apologize and complain. I swayed on my feet as he darted around me. I was afraid I would fall over and go to sleep and then wake up to find him gone, which would mean I'd have to run hard into a wall until I forgot about him. My head would need considerable battering to leak out the sense of this new, amazing man. The helmet would be required, and great gulps of the forgetting water, and a mouth packed with seeds while I slept. His energy was big and I had no part of it. I felt threatened by his happiness. I was too tired, and he was too fast to look at. Being with him was like being alone underwater—everything was slow; nothing counted; I could not be harmed; I would feel dry and cold when I resurfaced. No matter what was happening as his body blurred around me, I worried I might forget it all and have to be myself again, without ever having seen him. There was nothing for me to do but notice him as hard as I could, to notice him, to notice him, to notice him until I did not know what it was to even try to look at somebody without collapsing with exhaustion.

My pajamas were on the hook because I had the window closed and the wind was turned on high out in the world, making my room feel under attack, a bunker keeping the hard sound out. I kept twisting and the wind only got louder, until it was like getting breathed on so hard, it would make me older, with fast air that would turn me into my father. When Pal climbed on and found me with his mouth, I just couldn't stop laughing, but it was a laugh like an allergy, coming out too hard and strong and choking me, until I lost my breath and went down into the twisted sheets. Pal was part of my body now, but I felt even lighter. I had taken on a passenger, or he had taken on me. Together we were something less, which felt like such a relief, to not be ourselves for a while. I did not know where the rest of me had gone. We could creep from the room without sound. We could casually go to our graves. He would be my camouflage. I rolled over and silently laughed into the pillow, and Pal just sat on my bed on his hands and knees and he drove his mouth into me all day, telling a joke without words, one that tickled and hurt and never quite finished. He kept finding me out until he had solved me, and I was no more than a spill of water on my bed, a leak, soaking the sheets. I was only a bit of math for him to do, and then he had done me, and I was over, solved, finished. I had been answered.

I didn't start mouthing back until I was older. Jane Dark had moved in and set up her program—a great gymnasium of ladies laboring to be silent—so Pal came to live with us full-time. Father turned scarce, restricted to a shouting position some distance into the field. He raised a fist and yelled, and sometimes he threw a small wooden lance at the house, to little effect. I could imagine small birds breaking against the shutters. Pal and I spent our days in great schemes and chases. Pal would sit back with his legs up and yell at me, but I never knew what he meant. We wrote no notes. To make him stop yelling, I'd put my head down and charge like a bull into the wall. Sometimes I charged so hard, I couldn't stand back up.

Pal yelled louder. We yelled at each other and I tried to learn his language. I would take off my pajamas and play bomber with him, and Pal would calm down for a while, his face bristled and distant, breathing hard, as if it were a language of its own that I should study. I listened to his breath and heard foreign words an old man might say. Then I could approach him and he would pretend not to notice. I could make his breath go steady and slow, until there were no words in it, as if I were washing the air that came out of his mouth, polishing it into my own private wind, until it was a word so pure, it sounded like nothing at all. We would run down near the fainting tanks and sometimes we would play dead for whole afternoons, sprawled next to each other in the grass as if we had been killed far above and had just landed dead like that. When Pal played dead, he invited blackflies around his person, and they would commence to circle and dive-bomb at him. I could hear the whining pitch of their flight. Then he was all of a sudden up fast and running, the flies disturbed from their meal, Pal perfectly happy to have fooled them. I did not much care to stand up after playing dead. My body refused to work. The grass down there was so clean and cold and sharp—I felt plugged in to all those thin green wires. It was the best way to die. When I finally pulled myself up to walk home, all those wires were severed and I operated without power, trying to smile at Pal with my broken, run-down face, which kept slipping down my chest, begging me lower. Trying not to sink back down into the soft shore of the pond, where my face could stay buried.

When I went downstairs the day of Pal's first visit, my mother said I should wash my face, but she didn't wait for me to do it.

She was quickly on me with a sponge, roughhousing my cheeks, using the sandy side all over my head, until it chafed and strawberried. She showed me notes she must have scribbled while I was upstairs with Pal, admonishments of one kind or another. I was in for corrections. There would be new learning water to drink, new behavior flash cards, and gymnastics against emotion. An itinerary was written out for me with early rising times, and cleaning duty at the fainting tank. The ladies in the room applauded my mother, quietly patting their knees as they crouched like elders, and my mother just scrubbed me harder, as if she were acting in a play that required her to do this. I thought we were all watching ourselves being serious. I made a serious face and tried to look tired. I held my breath until my vision clouded and I felt older. She showed special vigor on that part of my head that would have had hair on it had I been more like other boys, buffing the very top of me. Some of the girls in the kitchen laughed, imitating me getting scrubbed up. They squinched their faces and dodged about the room, pretending to fend off the sponge. To everything I did, they invented a dance, so that even when I tried not to move, they exaggerated my stillness and strutted like stiff-limbed robots. The smallest girls in the background simply hissed through tiny perforations they made between their fingers, filling the kitchen with a young, female wind that was sharp on my skin. I thought my bones might slowly break. It was like being held by a large hand, choked by air that had formed a corset around me.

By the end of this public washing, I no longer had any of Pal on me, but I didn't need to; my heart was flushed and fast and I could still feel him in the fat wall of my chest, where I had decided to save my day with him, where he pulsed in me. My mother released her sponge to a group of girls, who quickly bagged it and marked the bag with code. The sponge was brought over to Jane Dark, who slipped it into her cloak and coughed.

They led me to the table. Dark wore a burlap hood and was muttering something. I felt happy; my face was clean; my vision had doubled, tripled, so I could see deep inside everyone, even all of the emotion removers, who were stone-faced and dead-looking, who had wept into cloth and laughed or raged into their hard swatches of linen that they wore in bracelets over their wrists. I could see inside Ms. Dark's hood and through her face and I could watch the tiny women struggling to operate this great lady's head, even though it was only blood and flesh like the rest of us, even though I only wished her design were something anyone could determine.

Dark took me on her lap, which was the first lap that I had been on. It felt designed for my own body, a seat only I could fit in. I rocked in it and it held me in a perfect mold, like a great warm palm. Mother looked on and turned her hand to some notes. She mimed a smile at me, but her face collapsed too quickly and I wasn't fooled. I still could not keep myself from smiling back at her, even though I had been told not to, covering my teeth with my hands. She would not hold my stare.

To everything I tried to say, Dark shushed me. I wanted to ask her about Pal, but she put a finger to her lips. When I mentioned that Father was outside, the whole room shushed me at once, the sound of a faucet turned on full. Dark held me closer and squeezed my torso, kneading my ribs and belly as if it were a dough, until I started to huff, just because it felt new so deep in my belly, especially when she held me like that. She placed her hand on me and I shushed the room in a loud expulsion. Little girls gathered near me and helped squeeze at my midsection until the shushing came from way down in my stomach, a silencing hiss I had not heard myself make before, loud enough to fill the room. The women all smiled and seemed shy. I shushed hard and long, with my eyes squinched tight, until my face felt swollen, as though a tourniquet were constricting my neck, and then the shushing seemed to release from my mouth and act on its own, and I could breathe quite separate from it and just listen to the hiss. It was so soothing that I was afraid for the kitchen to be quiet again. The quiet might hurt, without the shush filling the air like a great pillow. The quiet might tear something open.

We were all shushing, until it was a slow, steady hiss as plain as traffic. There had never been so much wind in that room, but no one was dying. My mother's smile almost seemed real. She looked like me, and I wanted to remember her. I tried to move toward her, but Dark held me close on her lap, digging her fingers into my hip creases so that I could only reach with my arms, and as I did so, my mother tilted away just slightly, as if a bug were too near her face.

Everyone laughed when my father came into the kitchen, a synchronized laughter that seemed planned, breaking up the steady hissing with hiccups of silence, so that laughing seemed like a fast argument between silence and hissing. My father's body looked small in the room. He was one of those fathers who died in a crowd. He tried to laugh and return the smile of these women he had never seen, but his face wasn't in it; it could not follow the command. I saw it slide down into a plain, father's face, a father who has a question or who is just resting his face in between times that mean something. The laughing smothered him, until he cast his head down at his feet to hide it, but his eyes stayed looking up at us, right under his eyebrows.

He was all messed about and dirty, rolled in soil. His shirt was torn and he had gotten too much sun on the sillier part of his face, as if he had fallen asleep curled up. What little hair he had was flattened and side-mounted up his face.

The women kept laughing, and Dark held me tighter. I pushed down into her lap and felt something poking at me. I looked at my mother. Her pencil was poised, but she was not writing. She was an accurate statue of a mother: so much detail, as if someone had made her. Her face was set in its control position.

My father tried my name out in the air, but the women would not stop laughing at him.

"Let's go now, Ben," he said. "Come on out here with me for a minute."

He shifted in the doorway, cheating his body out of the room, hinting how I should follow him. I could barely hear him over the laughter, but I saw him fading from the room, and it pulled on me.

Someone pushed my own hand toward my mouth. My father did not look at the women, only at me, and I saw his little mouth practicing my name so he wouldn't forget it, his eyes making no argument at all for anything. I wished my name were bigger and longer and louder in the room, so that my father would have something more important to say. Anyone could say a name like mine and nothing would change. As I tried to scoot off Dark's lap and go to him, she squeezed me harder, until it came from somewhere deep in my legs, a dry engine sound like rushing water. The laughing stopped, and it was only me in the room, the women squeezing my belly, one of my own fingers held up over my lips in the gesture of silence. The shushing posture. A universal signal for quiet. Directed at him in the doorway.

I looked right at my father and they squeezed me hard, triggering my hiss from deep inside me.

Nothing sounded. I bloated harder in my face, resisting their squeezing. The room was falling from sight.

"Ben?" my father asked again, and the word sounded like an apology a man might make before he died.

And that's when I could no longer hold the sound in. It poured out of my body hard and solid as water, a shushing that washed over my father and sank him.

There was no longer room for my father in that company— the room was allergic to his body and he would not be lasting long there. The women looked pleased by the suspense. My mother was suppressing a smile, her hand on her mouth, teeth shining through her fingers. Everyone regarded my father's little body faltering at the doorway as he took it in, until he backed out of there with small, chipped steps, looking down as he went.

Several of the smallest girls raced one another, giggling, to be the first to shut the door after him.

It was to be my father's last appearance in the house.

There was no thunder when Pal finally died. I had already forgotten about him. The sky did not look capable: too quiet, too weak, too far away to make any kind of sound we could hear. I found Pal in my room, crumpled in the corner like laundry. The toppled water jar against his mouth did not reflect any breath. Nor did my quick, hard kicks yield any flinches from his form. I touched his lips with some early sweet water he and I had made together, but his mouth was dry and finished. I poured a trickle of the forgetting water on his dry little head. Maybe he had died of memory. Maybe his feelings had caused an inner bursting. Maybe he had died of our house.

He was easy to pack in a bag. Just a bony container of hair. I stuffed him in and hauled him out of there, clomping down the stairs and limping into the field, glad to have so much to carry and somewhere to go, an errand elsewhere.

I exaggerated Pal's weight by plunging deep in my steps and miming gestures of great strain. I did the hernia walk. I panted, stopped, scanned the horizon, rubbed my muscles as if they ached. Several women were about their tasks, applying stethoscopes to the soil, but it was only Jane Dark who saw me lugging my product, Pal's bones jabbing through the bag at my back. I had not seen her with Pal for some time. Much was different from the words she had used. If Pal was a bomb, he was now defused. You killed my man, I thought. He died alone. You should die by thunder. You should be killed in a loud sky. Let your house break in half and the people inside it be pulled into the sky. Let you faint at night. Let your feelings drown you. Let my father return from the earth to hurt you with sound. She flipped down the goggles from her helmet and crouched in my direction, but if she guessed what I had in my bag, she showed no interest at all. Let you drive off in your truck. Let you never have come.

I left the compound, tracking through dried grass until

there was no more growth on the earth at all, just water, me, and Pal.

The pond was long and clean that day. Water ran in patchy sheets occasionally scored by wind. I could see just enough of my house in the distance, a shelter looking more like a sharp hole someone had torn in the horizon, pulsing with light, as if it might break open. For a moment, I forgot what was in the bag. It could have been anything, and I could simply have been a man that day visiting a thin stretch of water visible from his house. I had come a distance to do a job. That almost seemed to be enough. I had a bag of something, and would be returning home without it. But when I touched the hard bones, and felt the flat, plain face that once fit perfectly against the curve in my back, I knew whom I carried and what I had come to do.

No ceremony was necessary, no small words. I stepped up to the waterline and set the bag twirling over my head until its speed was sufficient to launch it well away from me over the pond. But I did not release it. The bag hummed in my hands until my arms were pulled taut, and I clutched it harder as the speed increased, feeling it drag my weight off the ground. I was not ready to let it go. I wanted true flight for this bag, not just an adequate throw, enough to send Pal deep into the water, plunging past the easy top layers into the true deepness, where a bolt of cold ocean water feeds the pond from below, where even a dead person might have his bones sucked through the backwash and out into the great wide ocean beyond, little bullets sent to sea. Pal deserved something more, even if I wasn't the person to give it to him. But I would try for him as if it were me in the bag, looking out through the mesh holes at the spinning world, cycling through trees and sand

and water and sky as I flew, until the water hit me like a wall and I could take a final break from the labor of breathing.

I twirled yet harder, until my arms ached, and then finally let my hands go, listening to the wind rip against the bag as it flew over the learning pond, where I had never buried anyone before. Pal could have been anybody up in the air, launched over the pond. My first body. My first throwing of a dead friend. I wished I were at my own window watching it all so I could remember it better, so that I could instantly faint it deep into my body. I would try to breathe less on my return home. I would try to swallow the feeling in my chest until it glowed in my bones.

The bag did not fly for long, considering what some birds do. But by the time the short, harsh splash had sounded, as plain as an old man coughing, I had turned my back on the pond and was already setting out for home.

My father would not be there. No one resembling a mother would be there. And now Pal would not be there. There would be people answering to names they did not deserve. It would hurt to say their names. I would head upstairs and crack the seal on a jar of tomorrow's water, next week's water, next year's thin, sweet water—going as far ahead into the future as I could, until the water was barely there, clear and weak and airy—and I would commence a fine, hard drinking spell, until this whole day, and the days before it, and then the people in those days and myself entirely, and my hard, dead name turned into a slick wire that pulled farther and farther away from me, slipping finally from view as I filled myself, as I took in enough water to make myself forever new to the small world that held me.

Blueprint

I AM PROBABLY BEN MARCUS. I might be a person. There's a chance I lived on a farm meant to muffle the loud bodies of this world, a sweet Ohio locale called Home, where our nation's women angled toward a new behavior, a so-called Final Jane. We could have had special water there, a behavior television, a third frequency, after AM and FM, for women's messaging, for women to steal the air and stuff it with their own private code.

Most likely I am still alive, suffering from a heart, unsatisfiable hands, legs that walk away. I may be the son of a woman who chooses not to move, refuses to speak. My father could be interred in a hole—the American word for his condition would be "buried"—punished for interfering with the women who called an end to motion and noise. My father may have stood up to himself and lost.

If I had really lived, I would have been the subject of emotion-removal experiments, person-blocking strategies (PBS), attempts to zero out my heart. It may have worked. Yet somewhere in the past, a period of time also called the mistake zone, it's possible a hardened creature with black hair, wrongly taken for a dog, took a leading role with my heart, walked me through a series of steps that ended up counting as my life, then left me in some after-house called Ohio, where I have nothing to do but issue reports.

It's possible that I cannot hear, that my head will not admit sound. There is very little chance that I survived.

System Requirements

This book is unfortunately designed for people. People are considered as areas that resist light, mistakes in the air, collision sweet spots. At the time of this writing, the whole world is a crime scene: People eat space with their bodies; they are rain decayers; the wind is slaughtered when they move. A retaliation is probably coming. Should a person cease to move, she would cease to kill the sky, and the world might begin to recover. Women seeking to increase their Mercy Quotient should follow the example of my mother and her cohorts by bringing a New Stillness upon their persons. They should read no further, for even reading is an embarrassing spasm of the body.

Although this book is for people in general, it is more specifically designed for people who have fallen over, who can't get up, whose hands hurt and eyes smart, whose limbs are tired on the inside, though doctors might find nothing wrong with them.

Healthy, sturdy, "strong people" (an oxymoron) are welcome to do their best to fetch this book into their persons through whatever word-eating technology they favor: reading, scanning, the poultice, a Brown Hat. But healthy, sturdy, and strong people probably don't need to be reading a book, do not miss anything in their lives that would make them want to waste time sitting down with a book that, admittedly, won't do much to add to their strength or confidence or well-being, properties that are probably cresting at an all-time high for them right now anyway. Such persons might find their assets diminished with this book, which in turn might lead this book to be seen as a challenge for those who are enlivened by threats of failure, people who have only ever thrived after being criticized, demeaned, misunderstood. In which case, this book can accommodate the healthy, sturdy, and strong people, but it may be an occasion of loneliness and confusion for them, though the whole notion of an "occasion" fairly thoroughly guarantees loneliness and confusion, and such emotions are not technically supported. Nor are any other emotions technically supported here. Readers looking to indulge in the having of emotions (HOE) should do so on their own time, in small bursts, preferably in a closed room, coughing often into an absorbent rag and wringing the rag down a drain.

But for the Limitations of Space

There should be pages of this book devoted only to women's weather, to Atlanta wind, to the women's radio frequency, to the mouth storm. A one-hundred-page section, with German references, should provide a final history of the American mouth. The American mouth would never need to be discussed again.

But for the limitations of space, more man-on-the-street interviews would have been conducted; a new technology for weeping would have been produced; a character named Steve would have died repeatedly at the start of each chapter. But for the limitations of space, this entire book would go without saying.

There should be a list of all the people who have walked the earth, or been seen breathing above it, their names and habits, the failures and successes of their hands. The list would be a pull-out parchment affair, embossed with small type. It would finally be a book that excluded no one. And then when all the world's people had been singled out and praised for their good works, forgiven their failures and near misses and broken promises, both to themselves and others, excused every digression of their hearts, when their names had finally been inscribed by wire onto a piece of wood that bands the earth like a belt holding the whole place together, these people would once and for all be killed, so that they won't return and won't be remembered, a complete killing in the old-fashioned style of the Ohio Exits, where not only the person is killed but the things around him and any referencing devices indexing, in any way, the person: killed. In a perfect world, these people would continue being killed until a zero population had been reached, until the cities and towns and other life-viable areas and elsewhere were just empty boxes free of people, and the phrase "free of people" could actually be uttered safely in every area and finally be considered true.

In a Perfect World
All the characters in this book should line up one by one and walk through a low-lit wood-paneled room, where you should be able to inspect their bodies, their hair, look into their mouths. You should be able to undress and handle them as though they belonged to you, pursue a casually confident inter-

course against their flesh without recrimination—unless you desire it; without consequence—unless it is part of your arousal apparatus to be blamed, held accountable, reproached.

Good books should offer characters for fondling, more characters for private and group fondling, in lakes and onshore, whatever sweet locale the customer chooses. In a perfect world, good books would offer characters with sparse, tear-away clothing and touchable bodies, sweet faces, skin that smells the way milk would smell if it were really the tears of God, just the most perfect kinds of people, provided by the very best books, so that we could finally stop the world of the book and fish the attractive people from it for our own private inspection, which even the best books have already denied us, though we are taunted with the most believable, palpable, and beautiful characters, who, no matter how real they seem to us, ultimately fail us miserably because we can never touch or fondle them, cannot fish them from fakery and thrust away all our frustration on them.

We should be able to grab whoever entices us and really get down to business on their bodies, doctor them, treat them, submit to them, play horse to exhaustion, dress them up or down, pose them, give them words to say that we have been waiting all of our lives to hear. People should be able to conduct their own private inspection of anyone they wish, to finally satisfy their curiosity with everybody out there that they could never hope to touch in the governable world, even if they don't know what they want and have never known. As long as the current laws apply, it would not be possible. In a perfect world, the current laws would not apply.

If I had my way, I would supply people for everyone to have

intercourse with, people that other people could tie or dress up, chase, undress, kiss, touch, squeeze, maneuver into position, throw off a horse and tackle and rough up, pamper, drape in cotton, in linen, in gauze, in cashmere, in fleece, rub with butter, cover in oil. I would have these people delivered every morning in a van or dropped off by trucks, sold on the street, displayed in windows, used as props in the park like public sculpture, except malleable, the way the very best bodies of this world are so malleable that we can actually break them for good, which is always what makes other bodies so treacherously joyful to handle, the fact that the people in this world are just so unbelievably and easily killable. If I had my way, I would be a purveyor, a sergeant of pleasure. In a perfect world, books would give more sexual pleasure. People would give more sexual pleasure. Sex would give more sexual pleasure. A storm would come and we could drop our trousers and finally really fuck the wind. We could leave our seizures everywhere; the world would be steeped in seizures, a cartoon world of spasming citizens. We could power the whole world by thrusting our hips into the weather. If we stopped thrusting, the world would slow to a crawl.

I Would Like to Help You

If you wish to fondle the author, I should take off my clothes for you and sit on a bed to the tune of a funeral march, or a sound track of your own choice, or no music at all, though I will warn you that my mother spoiled me for silence and my body sometimes fails to appear in a hushed room; I do not show up so well without sound. There should be mournful music and the smell of warm food, an unimpeachable day of fair weather, and you should be allowed your way with me, until whatever terrible insufficiency you're nursing has been soothed. At the time of this writing, I am nowhere near my ideal level of compliance. I should be so submissive that something will finally come true for you. You should take out your worst, your most secret fantasy on me. You should use me as a surrogate for whatever never happened to you, or whatever happened too much, or didn't happen correctly.

When you have exhausted your capacity for love or hatred or ambivalence, if there is any difference in these three daytime strategies, you may close the book. Only first tell me something special, a sweet thing only you can say, because as shallow or wooden or headless as I might seem, I still require a word of devotion, a cooing noise to comfort me, just anything soft and from your mouth alone. If possible, please also scratch or hold my head, because my head feels far too little held in this life. If I had to take my thousands of desires and their millions of horribly unquenchable offshoots and digressions and contradictions, most of which quickly leave the realm of law and sense and logic, and enter a place of pain and shame and impossibility (PSI), and from these innumerable desires choose only one that I would forever have addressed whenever and wherever I liked, in the cities and at the behavior farm or down in my father's cell, an instant satisfaction I could summon with a button, or the clap of my hands, that desire would be to have my head handled, to have it scratched and rubbed and cradled, washed with a soft rag, wiped dry if wet, moistened if dry, kissed, kissed, kissed forever, scratched, covered with fine stuff, the most expensive velvet, rich creams, discussed in discussion groups, analyzed by long-bodied men in coats, whispered about by girls from another country, never forgotten. I would simply and finally be happy to be able to snap my fingers or press the Give Me What I Want button, located ideally on my own body so that I could ask for love more discreetly simply by seeming to scratch my belly, and instantly have my head serviced whenever I desired, have girls and boys and their chaperones come running from their apology centers or fainting tanks to deal with it, a ritual as regular as prayer, where every member of a large city was constantly on call to deal with my head, full-timers, part-timers, temps, and scabs. If only my head could no longer suffer a boundary with other people's hands. If only there were no boundaries. If only my head and body didn't differ so from everything else. It is where my body begins to differ from what surrounds it that everything first seems to go wrong. If only my head were finally not my responsibility, could be put into someone else's care, could be made to merge with other persons and the world so that it would no longer suffer such distance and touchlessness, would no longer even be a head, because even when touched, there are parts of my head not being touched. Even underwater parts of my head feel dry.

If Things Had Gone My Way

I should still be alive in this book. I should not have died so young, or died at all, or ever been alive. I should have fought off my last failure of breath, been brave, said better things. There should not be a smooth wooden tombstone engraved with my name and planted in the field behind my Ohio home. The tombstone should not say RIP, or Here Lies, or Quiet Goes a Man, or Survived by No One.

I should be able to say hello to my mother, to wash my father's hands, to hear my mother sing a song, rather than imply it with her fingers. I should be able to breathe without the sky suffering from lack of birds. The air I make should no longer hurt the men and women. There would not be an empty room without windows in a perfect world. In a perfect world, nothing would have happened yet. Everything would go without saying. All of the sayings would be a given.

What's Inside

This book fails the Wixx/Byner comprehension test. This book eludes the Ludlow Plot Distribution Requirement Phase detection, which sleuths linear progression and character continuity in texts purporting to be fiction, of which only a small number actually are. By a wide margin, this book fails to meet the Coherency Requirement for Machinery Manuals as determined by the Ohio Clarity Foundation. The Reader Memory and Nostalgia Club, from Ohio, scores this book a six out of a possible twenty-five points, yet this book induced 415 false memories or recollections from the members of this club, who were prone to insert events from their own childhood into the plot of this book. This book required seven Simplification Batch Processes on the Language Cleaner Machine in order to render a legally binding one-hundred-word summary of its contents for the *Annual Brochure of All Texts*. The resulting one-hundred-word summary of this book proved too legally similar to the Declaration of Independence to be included here. The Reading Wizard, a machine that scans and summarizes books to determine their themes and content, determined that this book was "a documentary account of the role of the mouth in the art of deception and failure, with a specific focus on children who have been buried alive."

Statistical Data and Codes

The word "and" is often used as a secret code. It can be rubbed with the finger. Sometimes the word "and" serves as a distress call between two words or objects, which can often have no relationship without it. The word "heart" means "wind," unless it follows the word "my," in which case it can mean "mistake," in a world where weather functions as the combustible error produced by people, although sometimes the word "heart" indicates the social intermission people use to feel sorry for themselves, when self-pity is medically treated by vocal noises of certain volume (a type of song some bodies produce, called "sympathy").

Possibly the best kind of regret occurs between sentences, which may be why the word "shyness" is frequently mispronounced as "crevasse." "Wind," when used in a sentence, means danger. When used alone on a page, no interpretation of "wind" will be required, but the page should not be allowed to remain open in an unattended room. An unattended room is an empty room, or a room with someone's sleeping father in it. Sleep, when practiced by someone's father, is also known as The Penalty Box. A father, in this book, no longer affects the population of a town or peopled area. The population of a town is computed as the number of people minus the fathers. No other interpretation is any longer required of fathers. Slamming the book shut produces wind on the face, a weather that is copyrighted by the author, and this wind may not be deployed without permission, nor may the pages be turned without express written permission.

A misspelled word is probably an alias for some desperate call for aid, which is bound to fail. If "wind" is misspelled, for instance, as h-e-l-p, or i-t-h-u-r-t-s, then a storm can be expected, a hard sky, a short paralysis of rain. Rain is used as white noise when God is disgusted by too much prayer, when the sky is stuffed to bursting with the noise of what people need. If all the words of this book are misspelled, but accidentally spell other words correctly, and also accidentally fall into a grammatically coherent arrangement, where coherency is defined as whatever doesn't upset people, it means this book is legally another book. Likewise, if another book is comprised entirely of misspelled words that, through accident or design, happen to spell correctly and in the proper order the so-called words of this book, which in fact will be proven not to be words at all, but birdcalls, then that book might be regarded as a camouflage enterprise or double for this book, though it would be impossible to detect whether this were ever the case, in which case something is always a decoy for something else, and the word "camouflage" simply means "to have a family." In this book, the word "decoy" means "person." A person is always camouflage for something small and soft and possibly buriable. Often he should be killed to discover what he has been aliasing, even if it is just the most perfect thing: a person-sized piece of empty space.

Throughout the book, the names of children, people, heroes, gods, and things are generally given without accents, which are too personal to most readers (though other personal devices, such as women's names, have been retained), and the spelling of such names is mainly that which accords most nearly with Old American pronunciation as specified by the Ohio Diction Team, who are considered to have the ideal mouth shape. Spelling is a way to make words safe, at least for now, until another technology appears to soften attacks launched from the mouth. If we didn't spell them, they would hurt us more directly. The appearance of blood would indicate success. Spelling puts a corset on words, takes the knives out of them. Spelling a person's name is the first step toward killing him. It takes him apart and empties him of meaning. This is why God is afraid to have his name spelled.

Performance Notes

This book is meant to be recited at libraries with a pound of linen ballasting the inside of the mouth of the orator or nanny; no one else may legally recite it. Rest rooms should be stationed near any reading of this book, as should fatigue houses and guilt huts. Women's rest rooms should be guarded by a policeman wearing a gender helmet, even if such a helmet passes as a hairstyle. The doctor-to-audience ratio of a crowd listening to this book, by choice or by accident—since it is designed for recitation in public parks and heart-solving squares where unwitting customers of this book might be resting on blankets, waiting for their chance to feel nothing—should be 1:15 or better. This book sounds more clear, makes more sense, when recited through a megaphone, at night, under clear skies, in an area free of birds. When recited with a German accent, this book might induce crouching. A helicopter should be standing by at all times, unless the recitation occurs in an urban stadium within one mile of a hospital, in which case ambulances should be ready to cart the wounded to whatever local healing site obtains. A religious figure should be stationed near the site but not inside. Chances are that a religious figure will already be stationed there. If resources permit, for every hundred persons in the crowd, there should be at least one masseuse to rub and caress the listeners, using "literary hands," which assist a person who can't comprehend language. Public money should be used to deploy roving masseurs to caress citizens of our public areas so their bodies might better yield to the speech and weather broadcasts streaming from this book.

Behind the Scenes: An Inventory of Accidents
The author lost the use of his hands for three weeks while writing this book. During the period this book was written, he wept six times, one of which was used to secure sex as a sympathetic response to perceived sadness, a sex that produced in the author a diamond-cutter tumescence to his erection, leading him to conclude that weeping and arousal were intimately related, so that he often tried to weep before initiating intercourse, as foreplay; weeping became his most reliable seductive tool, at least for his own desire (because during sex he had first to seduce himself, an elusive and often unseduceable figure), though he was frequently merely alone to deploy his diamond-cutter, with two-person intercourse itself an imagined option at best, which he then concluded to be the actual best option, with real intercourse coming to seem contrived and imagined, ornate and implausible, too theatrical and overproduced, less vivid than the kind he conjured for himself in his mind, thus less realistic.

He became choked up 412 times while reading books, watching films or television, talking to friends or acquaintances or strangers or children or himself, or sitting alone in a house or park or person booth or public-transport vehicle, such as a police cruiser, unable to talk to himself or think or speak aloud. Indeed, becoming choked up became such a constant experience, as familiar as breathing, though no less unbearable or inaccurate a method to keep time with the world, that he no longer noticed it and came to regard it as his stable mood, one that held weeping at bay only tenuously and foreshadowed an emotional release just moments away, all the time, yet never actually delivered this emotional release, thus foreshadowed it falsely, or did so truly only six times, as mentioned, but the other 406 times failed to deliver any emotional release whatsoever, only threatened to produce weeping, but in the end managed actually to produce the reverse of weeping—a series of emotional captures—deciding that his own person was akin to a correctional facility for feelings, which had been placed in his body under house arrest, his body a manner of tomb, and that he was the warden of all the various ways to feel, though it should be remarked that these captured feelings were in no way rehabilitated for later release while serving time in his body. They were put away for good.

This man had a failure in his neck five times, which resulted in immobility of the torso and head and led to the use of an old foul-smelling neck brace once prescribed for him when these body failures were more frequent, then later used as a language diaper when uncontrollable speech was a symptom, a pillowy brace, shaped like a snake, that was saturated in all of his unwanted words, stinking of a version of himself he wasn't able to share with the world, wrapped around his neck, a towel for his secrets.

During the period this book was written, he tripped up a flight of stairs three different times, incorporating three different flights of stairs, striking his chin on a step a total of one time, scuffing either his right or left wrist a total of one time, but feigning injury all three times, behaving as though the stumble were intentional and part of his natural boundless energy, to bounce off stairs and even slap his face against one of them and find it all part of the bustly navigation everybody signs up for when leaving the house for the adventure, the disaster, of the daytime trajectory. All three times, this man looked back after stumbling, to see who might have seen him slip, noting their faces and names, if available to his sight, promising himself to hate them as fully as he could at the soonest possible occasion (an occasion he tried to design by aiming his body in their direction), through either indifference or direct aggression, or some yet-to-be-devised strategy, which he was eager to invent and deploy at these witnesses for having seen him in pain, seen him stumble, watched him fail at being himself, as though it were even possible that anything involving motion could ever be said to succeed, or that a person, especially a man, could actually ever be anything, not to mention something so directly impossible as being himself.

He fell, sometimes on purpose, a total of nineteen times during the period this book was written, and he told a story once after intercourse, to the person who had just politely and patiently hosted him while he hyperventilated in their shared space until his error had been registered as a small dollop of fluid he extruded from his mistake zone, of falling as a child and suffering a terrible blow to his leg, a story he then later came to associate with having intercourse itself. Any kind of leg pain thereafter made him desire sex, though the fall and injury depicted by the story occurred more than ten years before he had ever had intercourse; he was only a child when he fell, but the story became a dirty story, an erotic one full of promise, and it came to depict what he called his first sexual encounter, a run-in with the hard earth that damaged his leg, a story with secret pornographic implications that he often imagined represented in a full-color pictorial with children and a cool, suburban palette. He also told a story, just before intercourse, of falling from his motorcycle, and thus a motorcycle crash was for him the ideal depiction of intercourse, which was one of his first justifications for introducing a helmet into the bedroom.

Most of his experiences of intercourse were free of speech, or, more specifically, free of consonants, since vowels indicate pleasure and consonants indicate pain and confusion, and he pursued an Ohio Lovemaking Stratagem that focused mainly on his own pleasure, a sensation that was found to dilate if certain all-vowel exclamations were launched; his lovemaking was once endorsed by a mayor, which was also once his sexual nickname, "the Mayor," though it was admittedly a name he bestowed upon himself and never actually uttered aloud, except within the cavern of his terrible head. Yet because the people orbiting his mostly failed person proved entirely reticent to assign him nicknames or pet names or any kind of slogans or monikers or handles or endearments that veered even one letter from his actual name—even though in one sense all he ever wanted was to be someone with many nicknames; it seemed so exciting to be known variously, cutely, wrongly—he was obliged to take up the task alone and refer to himself quietly as "Champ," "Rip," "Daddy," and "the Mayor."

This author was called to perform bodily attention on six different women during the period this book was written. Of those six women, four of them unknowingly used a nearly similar vocabulary to describe the defects of the author, cited as: impatient, distracted, selfish, self-centered, dull. The other two women were similar in using nearly no vocabulary at all in describing the author, refraining almost entirely from the rhetoric of description or from any language that might have indicated any insight or interest in things involving either the author or otherwise, if indeed those are the only two choices of speech topics—the author or otherwise—since dichotomies such as that one still tend to present too complete a picture, and thus invite the worst kind of disappointment, that of knowing all of one's options. In short, the other two women refrained from language or excessive gesture or anything thought to pass for communication before, during, or after intercourse (the only three possible descriptions of time), though it is admitted that the absence of all communicative actions becomes, in itself, a rather forceful and unambiguous communication itself, interpreted by the author as: Get off of me, Get away, Don't touch me, Leave me alone, Stop, you're hurting me. The author has thus come to interpret silence, even his own, as a directive to cease and desist, to apologize, to enter the opening moments of behavior known as regret and shame. The author concluded that silence was a green light for shame.

As to the doubts the author experienced while writing this book, they were characterized variously as suspicions, regrets, and certainties. The phrase "known failure" was used most often in the early evening, generally muttered "under his breath," a technical impossibility, since at the time of this writing spoken language has yet to occur without breath, or under it or on top of it, despite the efforts of the female Silentists to deploy "words without wind." (The author concluded that for breath to occur without a word attached was a violation of what breath was for—namely and exclusively as a transportation vehicle for language, a small car meant to compete in the space normally reserved for birds and wind; thus breathing itself was considered the first language, and if the author breathed at all, he should always, at the least, be sure to layer a word into the breath, so as not to be wasteful with the vehicles he dispatched into the air, often choosing the word "help," for its simplicity and accuracy and full-time relevance.) He was openly admired for admitting his doubts, when confessions of weakness briefly passed for bravery, when certain persons in his life responded favorably to what the Ohio Pillow Talk Council calls "Fallibility Narratives": pre- or postcoital speeches that prove the superiority of someone other than the speaker and instill respect and empathy in the listener, thus possibly creating the desire for sex, when humility and self-deprecation are seen as a covert kind of strength, best responded to by a submissive presentation of an orifice (SPO).

Last Wishes

When the time comes, and the day has failed, and this book is finished or tossed away in disgust or quietly put aside after being just casually scanned and dismissed; when this moment arrives, if I should exit this place heading north, please let no one care to follow me or even watch my last body as it falls from sight over the hill. I prefer not to be seen or known or discussed. I should be given a head start of a ten-count. My enemies should be blindfolded and spun in place. There should be no wolves. When my execution is planned by the people assigned to kill me, wolves should be left out of it. Let no grief circles form related to my demise.

At the end of this book, the characters should stand in a line and bow. All the places and names should fade to powder. My father should walk across the stage and make a short ceremony of blowing the powder out into the faces of the audience, raising a chalky dust that clouds the air and settles like flour onto the audience. There should be no applause. People should go home wearing the decay that the book enabled.

The book should be closed so hard that a wind blows from it, gusting however feebly into whatever little world there is left. The day will be late, the sun a small accident in the sky, quickly apologizing from sight. This book wind will blow on whatever people happen to get in front of it, whoever's not too terribly tired to walk a short routine in the park and show off their body to the Bird. A shy breeze will rub their faces, twisting their hair into punctuation above their heads, the way wind from another town feels different and wrong and reminds you how far from home you are; some touch or gust or small warning of themselves, all from the wind released by this book, and briefly something will matter, though it will never be articulated or shared, but the wind will continue to digress, deflecting from bodies and objects, losing itself in the things of this world that pass for bodies and people, and the last little breeze from this book will finally fade out somewhere near the coast, where the land is dying every day into the water, just shy of the ocean, ending in a brief ripple in the sand.

If this wind were colored red, by a process that probably will get invented sometime soon, a cartoon weather to further exaggerate what goes on around us, lest we missed the point, in case some tiny fraction of life had miraculously gone unexplained, then the wind from this book would look like blood introduced into water, curdled and red and slow, a thick and terribly detourable fluid that can easily be diluted and absorbed invisibly into the larger world, and dissipatingly killed, by a simple wave of the hand.

There would be no funeral, unless a funeral can be characterized as a period of mass, united indifference; only a moment when everyone everywhere is all at once awake, in cities and in the country and even our enemies at sea, coincidentally thinking simultaneously of nothing at all in common, standing or sitting or reclining or diving, in an apparent world that is suddenly, and only for a moment, and for the very first time, completely free of air.

The tombstone for this book will read THE END.

Better Reading Through Food

My life has been lived under the strategic nourishment of the Thompson Food Scheme, a female eating system (FEAST) devised by an early Jane Dark deity construct named Thompson, who later became an actual person, though not a good one. The food regimen I have followed was further modified by my "parents" to suit their early experiments with silence and voluntary paralysis, not to mention the person-shaping projects they conducted on myself and my sister, who died for other reasons.

The diet Thompson and his food team developed was meant at first to favor a woman's mind and blood, to dispose her to the vowel world hidden within American dialects and weather, and lastly to enable strains of behavior considered to be distinctly female—actions, thoughts, and standing poses only girls and women can produce. It is also a diet meant to feed and promote silence, limit motion, and restrict hearing and speech to an all-vowel repertoire. In my own case, a symptom of selective deafness (to my father's voice, then later deafness to my own voice) emerged in my youth that I cannot help but relate to the food I eat.

Indeed, the word "eat" does not adequately cover what can be done with foodstuffs. For instance, I consume nuts in great quantities, as well as every kind of nut butter and the water extracted from pressed vegetable seeds, though the seeds themselves would poison me. I drink milk and sometimes take a syringe of pure, animal milk into a delicate vein in my ankle. In the morning, I chew the skins of fruit; the pulp is stored under my tongue throughout the day, then discarded into my chewed-food wallet, and later archived. I apply a fiber poultice against my legs, using a roughage sponge, and likewise use the meal of oats as a crushed paste under my arms or at the nape of my neck when I am fasting. In the evening, I spray my eyes with plant milk before retiring; this lubricates my blinking apparatus during sleep, throwing more light into my dreams, though I'm not much of a believer in the imagination. Every Sunday, I chew heated strips of linen, then stuff a handful of bleached soundproof linen in my mouth to prepare the area for food or speech purges.

If I'm going to say something important to my father, I'll fasten a tourniquet around my waist before I eat, to prevent lower-body absorption of the nutrients, which drives all of my bodily resources into my head in one huge rush, ensuring that my Dispute and Conflict Faculties will be fully charged.

Monthly, I cast a hot mold of my inner mouth, to catalog the changes to my palate, which helps me discern my purpose as a "person" and divine my next move in this world. The goal is to dilate the mouth cavity so that it can store more wind and inhale or alter the excess language in a room—since language is made, changed, and destroyed by air and man-made wind—although I would emphasize that I am not a word-eater. In the great state of Ohio, where I once had a home, there is a collection of Ben Marcus Palate Casts—also called Thompson Sticks, if the molding extends into the windpipe—that chart the structural changes to my inner head as I have trafficked into the present moment (huffed). My palate is shrinking and turning smooth over time, as certainly is my head, my hands, my heart.

I pursue food with my head and limbs wrapped in various fabrics, usually linen filters extracted from the Great Antenna—which increases the speech vitamins in my food, and primes my body to decipher women's radio waves, in case a command is given and Mother requires my help—but also cottons, wools, and rayons, burlap, and woven foil. I wear a helmet when I eat meat. If my diet requires bread or bread sticks or soaked dough, which it rarely does, or if bean oil, stew, or cake is indicated as a surface disguise or color filter for the object I'll be concealing in my body, I must take the nourishment while blindfolded and breathe into a cloth mouthguard for one hour afterward; otherwise, I'll die. Cheese is forbidden because it conceals accelerated milk. But I have farmed and eaten a cheese made from antique water samples left to harden and mold in my sister's wooden jewelry box. It's a translucent cheese with no nutrients or calories, but it animates the body during sleep and possibly improves deep listening skills. If something is being said, anywhere, I care to hear it. This cheese is also produced naturally in the hair of women who diet on girls' water and follow a promise of stillness.

If I wear a food bell, although I haven't worn one since my

father attempted a tonal study of my motion within our home, and the bell rings while I am eating, indicating a spastic posture toward the meal, a fast is required to slow my body's motion. When I was at my physical best, as a teenager, I could run away from Jane Dark if she or her assistants were chasing me—to enforce my copulative obligation at the Silentist compound—and I was frequently agile enough to keep the Ben Marcus Locator bell from ringing, even if it was fastened to my neck. I could run gracefully enough, though to many observers it appeared that I was hardly moving my limbs at all, arcing over the territory as if someone had thrown me.

Fasting is a common element in the Thompson Food Scheme, naturally, and it is fasting that will be recommended to the reader before setting forth into this book. The kinds of deep fasts, food-deprivation strategies, and language-cleansing styles certainly vary. Nor do fasts necessarily cause weight loss or decay of bone and muscle, although if I fast while listening to a recitation of all-vowel children's literature, I am prone to produce a small thread of human milk from my chest, after which I can be weary and given to fainting. Much of this boy's milk has been archived throughout my life and labeled in vials according to the genre that charmed it out of me. When I drink from the vials now, I can remember fondly those early stories of my youth: the adventures, mysteries, romances, and quest narratives that were converted by the Susan Group into an all-vowel format and hummed at me while I worked on the Great Antenna.

As a child of nine, I fasted for four months and still gained three pounds, accumulating mass through gestural practice and the hard women's mime that was popular at the time in my family. If I fast at the wrong time of day and become caught in a rainstorm, I could easily become paralyzed. I will never fast without wearing a heart magnet (also called The Cookie), which acts effectively as a reset button in such situations. In a winter water fast (wwf), the body absorbs water rather than swallows it, to ventilate the throat and mouth, and scour them free of language residue, or Word Sugar. Much water weight can be gained in the process; spot gaining can specifically be used to enlarge the hands (which can never be too big). When a dieter exits this fast, the French language is the only alphabet of sounds that will not wound the mouth, the flesh of which has softened under the absence of words and will be cut to shreds by the recitation of sharper languages such as German or English, at least until a palate callus is again developed so normal speech may resume.

As with most diets, however complex they are, water is still the crucial element that supports or undermines the actions of the various edibles. Water is clearly the primary instruction set for the person in the world. Yet Thompson Water™ is the only treated, strategic water used to forcibly alter and promote specific behaviors. (It is technically not a soda: When sweetened, it will burn through the belly and pass from the body as a photographic liquid of the person who swallowed it.) If used more widely in America, Thompson Water™ could easily lead to radical new behaviors—performances of the human enterprise never seen before. Such is the hope, anyway, of people like my mother, who distributed water in the most violent way imaginable (and whom I propose to reveal later in so much detail that no one need ever mention his mother again).

The notion of Thompson Water™ probably derives from the early American Pantomime Water (Shush), a liquid used to teach children how to behave in the home, marketed in a beverage series called Simple Skills for Children, at sixty cents a bottle. The inner Ohio Pantomime Water of the '60s, devised by Burke, was administered to me like baby formula and subsequently taught me how to stand and walk, to run, to read, to call my mother's name, and to sing using only mouth-carved breath, a storm music developed in Little England and used here to duplicate the sounds of trains, automobiles, and crashing waves. Despite everything that has happened, and everything I desired to happen that never did, I can still soothe myself with this kind of music. Pantomime Water operates under the principle that water is the purest medium to store the details of behavior. When my mother placed a jar of water in the Learning Room and then walked circles around it, the water recorded the principles of walking—it witnessed and reflected her motion—so if I drank from the jar, I absorbed the instructions and could then walk myself. The implications of this type of water-based instruction—to drink the source code of any task—are quite broad, and should soon lead to a widespread behavior-sharing system that will eliminate most notions of expertise and special skills. Basic tasks like mowing, painting, fishing, and hunting will be made available as affordable soft drinks. There will be men's water and women's water, water for sleeping, running, and hiding.

Because I am a man, the effects of the diet have not been optimal, to say the least. My beard has been slow to grow, I suffer a hollow feeling in my bones, and mostly I prefer to rest in my chair and watch the clouds bleed in and out of the sky. My parents probably understood this going into their project with me. Yet my career as a person has been aimed in part to shatter my accidental manhood and create, in its place, something else. I cannot resent being a subject for the food work and motion studies of men and women who are less than scientists, who are at the forefront of a field that hardly exists; while some of their errors and blind experiments have caused me direct pain and confusion, elsewhere their brilliant and pioneering work has ensured that my life has been filled with astonishing surprises.

While I do not presume to possess the food knowledge of a Thompson or a Burke or a Dark, or even someone as deeply wrong-minded about food and other mouth-destined objects as my imprisoned father, I have field-tested this book with control groups under the influence of varying food-combination/ absorption strategies, with and without water, in varying climates and stress conditions, and I believe there is a clear-cut way to optimize the reading experience, an eating program to best dispose the reader's body toward a story. Because my results are not statistically valid or verified by any literary council, I cannot say definitively that readers will necessarily survive the project I propose for them, nor am I interested in such a guarantee. Every eating style courts its own danger, and reading without protective equipment is risky for other reasons. Thus all food-intake recommendations, nonfood-nourishment strategies, special language fasts, and reading-equipment suggestions that I will offer are only meant as general guidelines and should not be undertaken without consultation with a doctor. Most American and English-speaking doctors will be familiar with the risks of food-assisted reading, and they will be able to offer advice tailored to the frailties of each patient.

The Fast

Because the Marcus family, through elaborate trial and error, bloodshed, and heartbreak, believes that food plays an important role in how words enter the body, and what these words come to mean, it is first recommended that a cleansing fast of nuts and milk be undertaken. For one week, nothing but these foods should be consumed; each day no more than a pint of milk and a pound of nuts. While an ideal reading experience cannot be guaranteed, the nutritive ballast of nuts and animal water can ensure that the reader's body will be sensitized to the women's histories offered in this book.

Nuts, when consumed in bulk, create a grammar sympathy quotient that is nearly off the map; almost any idiom can be understood through the regulated intake of these items. Although I have not been trained in the language of other people—the so-called French, Spanish, or Italian tongues, among others—I discovered early in life that alterations to my diet could help me understand the strangled noises of these people, should they ever decide to speak to someone like me, or should I ever be required to decipher their weird marks on paper. These alterations often involved a nut called the almond.

Milk, on the other hand, if properly prepared and consumed, increases sensitivity to unusual locution, dialects, and accents, while flat bread baked in hot salt for a day can aid with problems of believability, when the statements being made are incredible or impossible-seeming. Increased gullibility, on the other hand, is a problem with this type of bread. Liars will have a free run of a crowd that feeds in such a way.

Once the fast is undertaken, a healing crisis should come on the third or fourth day. For some readers, the crisis will be revelatory, with great understandings washing through the body like a wind made of warm water. Others may find the physical changes too abrupt and uncomfortable, and they would do well to stay near a private soundproof bathroom, or wear limb mittens to prevent excess spasm, seizure, and Infant Language Recall. (My first experience with this type of fasting proved to be too much for my small intestine, which ended up a casualty to the project—a language diaper is now required.)

Once this fast is completed, the tongue should be dry and hard, allowing spoken vowels a dynamic range and crispness that will compensate for a decreasing ability to produce hard sounds. It will be possible, in effect, to speak intelligibly with an all-vowel repertoire, rather like holding the tongue while talking. This new, women's language (since women's mouths are far better suited to it) has probably five times the sophistication of the crude, hard men's language known as English, filled with its rough consonants and abrupt acoustical stops, which inevitably result in the choppy air so prevalent whenever a man is speaking, the men's weather that, quite frankly, can start to stink, halting the flow of sweet air around a person's head.

Phase two of the diet begins when the tongue is hard enough to produce a clear knocking tone when addressed with a small mallet. This indicates that the mouth is ready to be filled with linen. The cloth recommendation here is not strict, but the dieter would do well to avoid wool and wool substitutes. The psychological setback would be too great, and I would no longer be of help through the many discomforts that wool-assisted reading might elicit. In addition, a dieter would sacrifice the claim to free technical support while reading this book if wool is used to stuff the mouth at this stage. Cotton may be used, but cotton does not wick away moisture, and it can thus prevent the full storage of the body's base language (which is nearly 95 percent water), in which case the language detox process would not be complete before reading, so there would still be sentence pollutants awaiting excretion. Cotton additionally begins to rot and expand if used as a language towel, whereas linen simply erodes into the earth. At any rate, enough cloth should be stuffed into the mouth so that the jaw extends to its full hinge and the cheeks appear ballooned. A neck brace at this time might also assist the dieter. The head, generally, cannot be supported enough, and shoulder splints may profitably be fastened up the ears to the level of the crown.

During phase two, it is difficult to take a full breath or to exhale around the obstacle of cloth in the mouth. Oxygen restriction while fasting (ORF) forces the body to derive oxygen from within itself, particularly from memories and extraneous behavior (which are highly combustible); unnecessary emotions are cleansed from the system through its natural furnace, and the body learns inner breathing. The primary use of feelings, in this book, will be as energy seeds for the body to burn, although the body, when gagged, needs to be trained to view these conditions as flammable. Fainting again becomes a danger here, so netting and helmets should be used to prevent injury. Indeed, a helmet should be worn *the entire time* this book is being read, and during any foray you might make into the world at large. A helmet will be one more barrier that could possibly save your life.

Food-Intake Strategies

Almonds are language-neutral. They will not affect the perception of sentences by the human head. Eating almonds additionally provides almost certain protection from fainting, which is a very real danger when reading this book. And although it will be demonstrated that repeated fainting is probably the purest way to permanently eliminate behavior, and thus rid the body of unnecessary emotions, it is not a career to enter recklessly. Strategic fainting requires equipment, preparation, and commitment, as well as a supportive family or diet team who are trained to catch and revive you when you collapse. Before I was ejected from Team Quiet, I was able to faint with regularity several hundred times a week, and stayed relatively free of injury (although my father would certainly disagree with this claim).

The Food

Directly before reading each morning, the reader should undergo a full-body flush, drinking at least one gallon of reader's water. Warm-up exercises should be light: basic limbering stretches, but nothing to increase the heart rate. If desired, a language enema might be taken (speak spontaneously until exhaustion, and your body will purge all of its unspoken messages and sentiments. It might prove useful to record this ceremony, as details about yourself can be discovered). Throughout the day, feeding can occur on fibrous vegetables and fruit, with occasional yogurt gargles and snacks of hard bread and butter. Since it is not recommended that this book be read in the evening, neither should any food be consumed during that time. Total rest is suggested and motion of any kind is discouraged.

For Advanced Readers Only

For those readers looking to optimize their time with this book (or people reading the book for a second or third time), the eyes should be masked in black cotton during the daytime hours of the fasting procedure and no other written language should be regarded. Thoughts, if necessary, should be conducted in shorthand or steno, and if communication is required, though I cannot authorize it (and in theory oppose it), a set of flash cards should be used, with easy-to-understand pictograms that will satisfy the demands of the basic interactions: commerce, expressions of love, hunger signals, and warnings of impending disaster. At the time of this writing, images are far less taxing than words and should be deployed anytime the head needs relief. If another book or pamphlet is placed before you and you are required to read it, which I cannot recommend, or if navigational messages are presented to your person during a period of travel (also to be avoided), a simple technique of nodding, squinting, and ducking should be used to quickly scan the message, which you would then do well to vowelize before it can take hold of your thinking in any substantial way.

Who Were the Jane Dark Gods and What Did They Want?

The first Jane Dark gods were invoked by members of Team Quiet in Ohio to solidify Dark's authority as a silence expert. Most organizations require a deity scaffold to boost their veracity with recruits. The deity referred to as Thompson has been used in fiction and nonfiction alike, and is not scheduled to die, or to suffer myth remission, until certain concepts have fully integrated the culture. The Jane Dark gods were never described physically, and they had no special powers.

Why Cloth?

My family believes that the inside of the mouth is equivalent to a cave. Words accrue and marinate as pockets of vibrational sound, changing the delicate structure of the palate, which influences the acoustics of spoken language, inevitably launching speech wind—an early form of menacing weather—into the atmosphere or deep into someone's body. Cloth is used not only to pad the surface of this cave but to absorb speech residue, to store the elemental messages of a person and delimit personal wind output (the Barking Quota). If every person carried a language towel such as this, much preliminary misunderstanding between people could be avoided. People could simply exchange language towels and chew them for instant, intimate knowledge of one another, rather like a peace pipe was once used, no doubt.

Does the Skin Eat?

It would be foolish to simplify the role of the skin in reading, thinking, and eating. Nearly everything that can be said about the skin can be disproved or at least convincingly denied. For the purposes of this book, once the fast is completed, the arms should be wrapped in the cloth you had stashed in your mouth. You are training your body to be a full-scale receiver of language, to feed on the noise of words as it does with so-called food. The sooner the head is decentralized in the nutrition-intake process, the more ripe the body will become to decipher nonlanguage communication streams like wind and electronic women's frequency. The skin should be frequently brushed with a wire scrubber to clear the pores; the skin of the arms might further be primed with a sixty-minute daily bath of high-volume radio static.

Why Nuts and Milk?

When milk is understood as *animal water*—a nutritive liquid produced by nonlanguage creatures enduring their brief term on earth—it becomes clear that this edible product of creatures allows us access to the bodies of strangers without risk, to steal their life information and expand our own possibilities as people. In this sense, milk is probably the primary learning water, a deep liquid that tells us how to act. It is precisely when I feel estranged from myself that I drink my own milk. Most men won't have this option. Their first choice should be another man's milk, or to cultivate milk from one of their male children. Nuts, on the other hand, can be derived artificially by a Voice Blizzard, in which hundreds of people speak rapidly (hark) into the same container until the vocal waves congeal, or "nut."

*What Is the Difference Between a Vow of Silence
and a Language Fast?*

In a language fast, cleansing measures and word purging accompany the quietude. A vow of silence is only an early step toward controlling the role of words in the head. Women's Pantomime, if performed according to Jane Dark's criteria, can sweat excess language from the body, accelerating the benefits of a vow of silence. A linen mouth guard, or any cloth gag, with the exception of a riding bit, might also allow the muted language to be stored and archived, for the purposes of later listening and self-study.

Should a Helmet Be Worn When I Make Love?

Until the notion of Helmet-Assisted Life catches on with more people, you may be seen as a threat if you wear a helmet during moments of intimacy. Yet it might also be true that relaxed intimacy cannot occur unless the head is fully protected. Desire is difficult to maintain during moments of risk and danger—men regularly attacked or humiliated by animals have frequently proven to be impotent. Perhaps the best solution is to encourage your partner to wear a helmet first, gently implying that it increases your arousal or fulfills a fantasy you've always had—that is, to make love to a beautiful person who is wearing protective headgear. Then when you introduce your own helmet into the bedroom, discreetly, of course, through a lights-out equipment-debut strategy, the helmet will seem natural and lovely, like a headdress once may have looked to warriors—honorable and sacred and sexual—and you can make love safely, without unwanted risk to your head. Helmets should slowly become a regular feature of life. Until that time, users should respect those people not yet accustomed to them, who still prefer a naked, vulnerable head.

Caution

The author discourages travel and indeed all extraneous motion during the reading period, both of which will tend to minimize the sympathy/fascination quotient by increasing circulation and allowing outside events to shape the emotional palette. A reader's sock, to immobilize the body while the book is being read, is the ideal harness. I favor a Smart Noose, which flushes my head to an itchy but excitable degree of swelling, allowing every word I hear or read to tickle me deeply at the back of my head. Other readers have used coffins, straitjackets, or have employed "the pinch," to temporarily paralyze themselves for the duration of the reading period.

———

The reading of this entire book should profitably occur over the period of one week, although "Kevin R." (not his real name), from Denver, took nearly a year to finish the book, and "Deborah," from the North, read it straight through and finished in nine hours, mostly because she could not endure the stricture of the reader's diet (due to a vomit response to language). These extremes in the reading duration are not encouraged. Indeed, both of these participants are still suffering from vertigo, rapid weight loss, and a flattening of the vision. I have attempted to correct their diet and offer language antidotes; children's verse, vowelized, seems to be the most effective, along with dry morsels of shortbread. (The stories of Hans Christian Andersen, recited without consonants, appear to relax and rejuvenate most American people.) Yet I cannot say with certainty that these readers will ever fully recover.

As for the reader participants "William L.," "Roger K.," "Sandra S.," and "Angela B.," I offer my condolences and apologies to their families. May they rest in peace. They were heroic young people, the bravest of readers, and they will be sorely missed.

Dates

1825

THE FIRST DOCUMENTED INSTANCE of the Female Jesus appears
in England in the form of a seven-year-old girl. Using rapid
clapping and tongue clicks, the girl lures various species of
birds from hundreds of miles away, who assume a circle of
protection around her and raise a field of sharp wind in the area.
When her father attempts to rescue her, the birds are able to beat
out a rudimentary language of ricocheted wind to command his
own hand against him, and he dies, a suicide. Several male witnesses also die, and the air that the birds have stirred with their
wings remains sharply turbulent at the seaside site for the next
five years, repelling any men who try to approach. This form of
barrier comes to be known as "Jesus Wind." It will be used
against men, together with a clear sock covering women's heads,
to neutralize their language at the End of Sound protest in 1974.

1922

Finland proposes a separate language for women, becoming
the first European nation to do so; all men and women twenty-

four years and older not considered suicide risks are fitted with a Brown Hat, to enable or prevent them from performing the new language. The Brown Hat, in women, is fitted into the mouth to allow a broader range of vowel production, which is considered a vastly unfulfilled potential of women (see *The Vowelists,* 1940). The flesh-colored apparatus is meant to camouflage the head. For a time, it becomes a symbol of status and wealth; streamlined designs create striking new possibilities for the human head, accentuating its animal shape. Women in Finland seen without the facial gear are considered incompletely attired and are refused admission to the black-tie Head Theater conducted in the countryside. Men are to utilize a smaller, darker Brown Hat (the Carl Rogers Cage), resembling a bridle, which will restrict their vowel production and crimp the skin of the upper face to narrow the ear canals, deafening them to the new language. Both men and women will be advised to speak nightly messages of personal import into a cloth screen that will be used to test for a possible chemical element of language (see *Language Poultice, Shame Towel, Prayer Rag,* 1962). No chemical difference is discovered between the speech of the sexes, only a marked absence of water in each, which will prove to be vital for later projects of the Listening Group, who will add water to its language filters, Brown Hats, or Thompson Masks in order to scramble or falsely translate their speech.

1928

The American Naming Authority, a collective of women studying the effects of names on behavior, decrees that a name should only have one user. The nearly 1 million American users of the name Mary, for example, do not constitute a uni-fied army who might slaughter all users of the name Nancy, as was earlier supposed, but rather a saturation of the Mary Potential Quotient. Simply stated: Too many women with the same name produces widespread mediocrity and fatigue. A competition of field events, centering around deployment of a forty-pound medicine ball into hoops and holes, is proposed to determine which women shall rightly hold the title of their name, with all losers in the same-name category to be desig-nated as helpers—subsets—of the winner, forced to wear wind socks or hip weights to slow down their progress, enslaved to the first Mary, the first Nancy, the first Julia, as the case may be. Parents still able to name their children begin to seek either unique names or names that are considered neutral by the authority, such as Jesus and Smith. Many girls are given the name Jesus Smith, which, when pronounced as an all-vowel slogan, becomes a crucial new word in the Silentist movement, and is also possibly responsible for enabling the new strains of female behaviors seen at this time.

1935

Boston widow Claire Dougherty is arrested on her doorstep October 3 by detective Sherman Greer as she tries to swallow a coded message. In prison, she refuses to speak and appears to suffer at hearing any kind of sound, a condition termed Lis-tener's Disease, in which even sounds produced by her own body appear to cause her agony. She must wear a soundproof suit and a life helmet. State doctors report that there is nothing unusual in Dougherty's hearing, but they agree to relieve her with a quiet cell in the prison and a full-body muffle, later termed a Claire Mitten and worn by young girls who are sickened or distraught at the sound of their own voices. Before she dies, in November, she writes in a letter to her daughter that "... a new sound is upon the world. We have erred greatly and will be killed for it. Look to the soil, for the sound to me was beneath it. Walk slow or do not walk. Hide. Duck. Listen." Detective Greer, the arresting officer, will die a year later, complaining of a "sharp noise" in the water near his home. His cause of death is listed as exhaustion. The two deaths will launch several studies of diseases caused by sound, and Greer's wife will later appear in the streets of Boston wearing an executioner's hood. Her body, upon examination, will reveal heavily damaged ears.

1942

A woman is found collapsed in a field, her arms sheathed in metal sleeves, nearly burned down to the bone. Her mouth is void of teeth and likewise charred. When a microphone is held to her skin during a routine exam by a Listener, muted voices and noise can be heard, suggesting her body has been crushed or otherwise altered with sound. During the same month, a caravan of women is intercepted by the Texas Mounted Police. Among their possessions are found a set of foil-lined sleeves and leather hoods, which the women will only say are used to "fight sound." When they are addressed during a group interrogation, they use quick actions with their hands to nearly silence the questions coming at them. The turbulence they generate with their limbs is recognized as Jesus Wind. They are apparently able to quiet the local sounds in a room simply by making shapes with their hands. A child Jane Dark is among them, who demonstrates that by standing next to a passing train and engaging in an odd form of gymnastic pantomime that appears part karate, part dance, the girl can mute the forceful racket of the train so that it passes by in virtual silence. Late in her life, it will be this talent that will prevent her from hearing even her own voice, as the orbiting wind of silence she herself has created becomes so potent that it can no longer be penetrated, and she appears to the people around her as a character in a silent movie. She can neither speak nor be spoken to, a deprivation of language that causes her hands to wither.

1952

The Women's National Pantomime group gathers on an athletic field in Dulls Falls, Wisconsin, for their largest event since their inception in 1946. Fifteen new gestures are introduced by the group leader, a slender teenager named Jane Dark, and so many women suffer seizures and vomiting after performing the difficult new movements that the local hospitals cannot contain them and Ms. Dark is forced into hiding. Four women die, while many others turn in their memberships in protest. The wounded women are so disoriented that they must relearn basic movements such as walking and kneeling, drinking and sleeping. The men's chapter of the Pantomime Association publicly renounces Dark and her followers, calling her modifications harmful and contrary to the chief purpose of Pantomime, which is to entertain. Dark explains that her fierce group of aggressively silent women will no longer exist to glorify the "false promise" of silent motion, or Pantomime, but will instead attempt a new system of female gestures, to replace sound as the primary means of communication, declaring motion the "first language," with a grammar that is instinctual and physical, rather than learned. It will be the first instance of a women's semaphore that will not be an imitation, but, rather, a primary behavior with, according to Dark, "very real uses in this country." Dark will begin authorship of a series of pamphlets called *New Behaviors for Women*. The pamphlets argue that gesture and behavior alone can solve what Dark calls "the problem of unwanted feelings." She also helps market Water for Girls, small vials of "radical emotional possibility," under the premise that water contains the first and only instructions for how to behave in this world.

1960

The English language is first overheard in a wind that circles an old Ohio radio operated by an early Jane Dark representative. Words from the language are carefully picked out of this clear wind over the next thirty years and inscribed on pieces of linen handed out at farmers' markets. When the entire vocabulary of words has been recovered from the radio, it is destroyed, and the pieces of linen are sewn together into a flag that is loaned out to various Ohio cities and towns, where it is mounted over houses. Once the fabric is hoisted on a flagpole, the language is easily taught to the people inside of their homes, who have only to tune their radios to the call sign of the flag station, extract and aim their freshly oiled antennas, and position their faces in the air steaming from the grille of their radios. When their faces become flushed and hot, they can retreat to other rooms and say entirely new things to the children who are sleeping there.

1965

A noise filter is created at Dark Farm to muffle radio and television frequency. It will be the first nonsacrificial attempt by Jane Dark and her followers to mute the noises of the air and bring about a "new world silence." Mounted upon the roof of a hilltop barn, the filter is a dish-shaped sieve filled with altered water that will supposedly attract and cancel electronic transmissions, including television, radio, and women's wind. The water, which absorbs the intercepted frequency, is considered a master liquid of supernutritive value. It is removed monthly and administered to the women as a medicinal antibody. The drink is called a "charge," or Silent Water, said to render women immune to sound.

1985

Quiet Boy Bob Riddle constructs his home weather kit, to definitively prove that speech and possibly all mouth sounds disturb the atmosphere by introducing pockets of turbulence, eventually causing storms. By speaking into the tube that feeds the translucent-walled weather simulator, which resembles a human head—in this case, the head of his father—Riddle demonstrates the agitation of a calm air system. The language that Riddle introduces to the test environment—whether English, French, or the all-vowel slang of the Silentists—repeatedly smashes the model house within, proving that sound alone can distress and destroy an object. His essay, "The Last Language," argues for an experimental national vow of silence, claiming that spoken language is a pollutant that must be arrested, first by stuffing the mouths of unnecessary speakers ("persons whose message has already been heard") with cloth. Before his death, in 1991, he will build a mouth harness (the Speech Jacket) that limits its wearer to a daily quota of spoken language, beyond which he or she must remain silent until the next day, or else trigger a mild explosive that will destroy the mouth. The Speech Jacket is tested first on children. Although it causes intermittent blackouts and fainting, it serves to restrict their speech to requests for food and short displays of all-vowel singing.

The Name Machine

I'll not be able to list each name we called my sister. The process would be exhausting, requiring me to relive my sister's pitiful life. There are additionally copyright issues connected with persons that are officially the holdings of the government, which is still the case with my sister, despite her demise. To reproduce the precise arc of names that she traversed during her life in our house would be to infringe on a life narrative owned by the American Naming Authority. It will suffice to select those names sufficiently resonant of her, ones that will seem to speak of the girl she was rather than of some general American female figure, although it could be argued that we can no longer speak with any accuracy of a specific person, that the specific person has evolved and given way to the general woman, distinguished primarily by her name.

The names defined here derive from a bank of easily pronounceable and typical slogans used to single out various female persons of America and beyond. A natural bias will be evident toward names that can be sounded with the mouth.

The snap, clap, and wave, while useful and namelike in their effect (the woman or girl is alerted, warned, reminded, soothed), are generally of equal use against men, and therefore of little use here. Gestures of language that require no accompanying vocal pitch, such as gendered semaphore, used in the Salt Flats during the advent of women's silent television, or Women's Sign Language (WSL), developed in the '70s as a highly stylized but difficult offshoot of American Sign Language, now nearly obsolete because of the strenuous demands it placed upon the hips and hands, were never successful enough with my sister to warrant inclusion in the study. She plainly didn't respond to the various postures and physical attitudes we presented to her—our contortions and pantomime proved not theatrical enough to distract her into action. No shapes we made with our hands could convince her that there was important language to be had in our activity, and she often sat at the window, waiting for a spoken name, without which she could not begin the task of becoming herself.

This is certainly not to imply that communication between persons and living things requires tone or sound, or that deaf figures of the female communities can have no names. There is always written text, to be apprehended through visual or tactile means, as well as the German-American technique of "handling" the name of a woman onto her thigh. My sister, as it happens, did not respond in any useful way to our repeated and varied handling of her body. As rough as we were, it made no apparent impression on her.

Here the American female name is regarded as a short, often brilliant word. Rarely should it inaccurately capture the person it targets, and its resistance to alternate uses, modifications, translations, and disruptions is an affirmation that individuals can and should be *entirely defined* by a sharp sound out of the mouth—these definitions have simply yet to be developed and written. Once they are, we will know what there is to know about all future persons who take on one of the appellations listed in the American Bank of Names, striving in their own particular way to become women of distinction.

Nicknames, admittedly, allow for a broader range of fetching, commanding, and calling, but the nickname only indicates an attribute or device of a person, such as the length of her legs, the way she sleeps, how she bounces a ball (in this case: "Sticks," "Taffy," "Horse"). A name, as the government instructs, can no longer be an accessory of a person, but must be her key component, without which the person would fold, crumble. She would cease, in fact, to be a person. The nickname, and more particularly the endearment ("Honey," "Doddy," "Love," "Lady"), speaks to a deeper mistrust of the original name, a fear of acknowledging the person at hand. If it is possible to change a person by changing her name, why not employ a name of diminished potential and thus diminish or destroy the person? It's a valid concern. When a man modifies or adorns a woman's name, or dispatches an endearment into her vicinity, he is attempting at once to alter and deny her, to dilute the privacy of the category she has inherited and to require that she respond as someone quite less than herself. (Conversely, women who are scared of their own names are also typically afraid of mirrors.) The movement toward a single name for the entire female community ("Jill," "James," "Jackie")—as aggressively espoused by Sernier and practiced by his younger employees—would disastrously limit the emotional possibilities for women and, rather than unify them as the Bible claims, probably force a so-called girls' war in their ranks.

The task of my family in this regard was to process and unravel the names that arrived in the mail, then dispatch them onto my sister, generally with the naming bullhorn, a small seashell my mother carved for the purpose. We were enlisted by the government to participate in what was being called the most comprehensive book ever attempted, a study meant to catalog the names of American women. In the book, each name is followed by a set of tendencies that are certain to arise if the user employs the name as the full-time slogan for herself. The book is meant to serve as a catalog of likely actions, not only to predict various future American behaviors but to control them. If the government regulates the demographics of name distributions, using a careful system of quotas, it can generate desired behaviors in a territory, as well as prevent behavior that does not seem promising. It's not exactly a style of warfare as much as it is deep dramatic control over the country. The book remains unpublished, but its authors are reported to be numerous, somewhere in the thousands, each working blind to the efforts of the others. In my possession are only the notes taken during the naming experiments on my sister—an intuitive set of definitions of the names she inhabited. We were not instructed how to define the names we were given, only to use them, study them, employ whatever research we could devise. I therefore have no notion if our material was ever incorporated into the text. We submitted it promptly but never received word on the matter.

We served up the names to my sister one by one and

watched her change beneath them. Researchers here might say that she became "herself" or that it was her body expressing its name, as if something does not know what it is until the proper sound is launched at it. Each new morning that she appeared before us and we announced the name for the day through the bullhorn, we saw her become the new girl and release the old one, drop the gestures and habits and faces that the last name had demanded of her and start to search for the necessities of the new name.

I presume that other men launch their childhoods with sticks and mitts and balls, skinned knees, a sockful of crickets, and other accessories. They are shoved onto a lawn, where they know the routine, can find the snake or book of matches, sniff out water, or sit in a children's ditch and watch the sky with their light and delicate heads. But I was the designated writer among us, unable to walk across grass or throw or catch or hide, equipped only with the stylus and pad, made to create our life in the form of notes on a page. This was unfortunate, because I don't like to write, I don't like to read, and I like language itself even less. My father read to me as a boy and I was mannered enough not to stop him. It was unbearable—book after book that failed to make or change me, my father's lips twisting and stretching during a supposed story hour, massaging a stream of nonsense inside his mouth. I have always tried to be polite about words—good manners are imperative in the face of a father wrestling with a system that has so clearly failed—yet I find language plainly embarrassing. It is poor form, bad manners, that so much hope is pinned to such wrong sounds out of the mouth, to what is really only a sophisticated form of shouting and pain. It is not pleasant for me to hear "foreign" languages, either. All languages are clearly alien and untrue, and, absent of so-called meaning, it is repeatedly clear that language is a social form of barely controlled weeping, a more sophisticated way to cry. To speak is to grieve, and I would prefer not to listen to a weeping animal all day and every day, sobbing and desperate and lost. Particularly when that animal calls itself my father.

Each time we changed my sister's name, she shed a brittle layer of skin. The skins accrued at first in the firewood bin and were meant to indicate something final of the name that had been shed—a print, an echo, a husk, although we knew not what. They were soft in my hands, devoid of information, and quite like what I always thought was meant by a "blanket," a boy's little towel, something to shield me from the daily wind that got into my room. It is not that the skins resembled a person anymore, or stood for one, or acted as a map of the past. They were, rather, a part of my sister I could have to myself—soft, foldable, smelling of bitter soap, perhaps like a toy she might have used. I kept them for hand warmers, penciled my pictures into their flaky surfaces, draped them over my bedroom lamp for spidery lighting effects and the whiff of a slightly burnt wind. Maybe I smelled something deeper as the skins burned away on the bulb, floating in and out of the cone of light that enabled my infrequent passage from bed to door, at such times when my bedpan was full. There was nothing of food to the smell, only houses, hands, glass, and hair. And her. They smelled of her.

Oddly, these skins my sister shed seemed to serve as a repellent to my sister herself, as if smelling her own body were uncomfortable for her. She would not come near my room when I was using them. Nor would she approach me, particularly if I wrapped myself in parts of her old body and walked through the halls, or bathed in a caul of her husks, which would cling to my skin in a gluey callus when they were wet. No one, I would venture, likes to be understood as deeply as I was understanding my sister at that time, shrouding myself in the flakes of her body that she had lost, wearing her. She preferred, I assume, not to know me.

When the names ran dry, my sister pulled up short somewhere in the heart of the Learning Room. The mail had ceased, and no one was sure what to call her. She slept on the rug and scratched at herself, looking desperately to all of us for some sign of a new name, of which we had none. No one, as I mentioned, was sure what to call her, a problem that proved to be the chief void in her identity, which slowly eroded. There were no more skins, and one morning my sister lost her motion and folded into a quiet pose. Out of sympathy, we reverted back to her original name, or one of the early ones. I have to admit that I'm not sure what name she began with. Nor were any of us too sure, to be frank, whom, exactly, she had become.

[Lisa]

Because the word "Lisa" most closely resembles the cry heard within the recorded storms at the American Weather Museum, a crisply distorted utterance claimed to be at the core of this country's primary air storms, the girl or woman to carry the burden of the Lisa name carries also perhaps the most common sound the world can make, a sound that is literally in the air, everywhere and all the time. (Most wind, when slowed down, produces the sound "Lisa" with various intonations.) The danger is one of redundancy, and furthermore that a woman or girl cruelly named Lisa will hear her name so often that she will go mad or no longer come when called. Children learn that repeating a word makes it meaningless, but they don't know why. Briefly: Weather in America occurs through an accumulation and disturbance of language, the mildest form of wind. To speak is to create weather, to supply wind from a human source, and therefore to become the enemy. The female Silentists are silent primarily to heal the weather, or to prevent weather, since they believe that speech is the direct cause of storms and should forever be stifled. A Silentist regards the name Lisa as the purest threat, given that, when heard, it commonly indicates an excess of wind, an approaching storm, possibly the world storm. The name Lisa, to some Americans, is more dangerous than the words "fuck" or "fag" or "dilch." It should probably be discontinued. It can crush someone.

Statistics for Lisa: An early name of my sister. She rarely acknowledged it. It caused her anger. We could pin her to the floor with it. She drank girls' water and would peaceably wear a Brown Hat. Her Jesus Wind resistance was nearly zero. Rashes and facial weakness were frequent. A distressed tone to her skin. Her language comprehension was low, or else she showed selective deafness. A growling sound was heard when she wrote. She seemed blind to my father.

3

The Technology of Silence

———◆———

Failure to Mate

The New Female Head

Women's Pantomine

Dates

Names

Failure to Mate

When I was first put to sire for the Silentists, my father, the senior male, had just been rendered into the hole, and no other youth were sufficiently available to dispense completions into the selected women. Maybe there were boys from middle Denver who coupled with some silent girls brought in by Jane Dark and Quiet Boy Bob Riddle, but I am to understand that I was the chief agent of physical contact among the various women's militia that came through town, even the Listening Group, who were loud and often took me with force.

The siring period lasted a full winter. My location was frequently the upper floors of the house. Toward the end of the copulative term, I waited naked on my father's surrendered bed, a denim ringlet assisting my erratically operative genital arm, an appendage referred to in my mother's notes as my "error." The chosen girl at her most fertile moment would make a slippered approach down the long hallway, often goaded along by Dark right up to the doorway, where she might balk until pushed into the room and onto the bed. She'd find me disrobed there, positioned on my back in the snow-angel posture, as instructed. She might gather up her dress and sit across my hips for the transaction. Sometimes she struck a sidesaddle position for efficiency, or T-crossed me, with her bottom smiling toward my face, always averting her eyes from myself or my body or my props. She may have worn a hood or blinders, a mouth-guard, a helmet. A linen jumper possibly covered her body. She was gentle and tall, or small-bodied, with clumsy hands that smeared my chest with some sort of listening grease if she lost her balance and fell onto me. She was shy or loud, mocking or rude. She had learned to move so silently that she seemed delicately afloat, using a cautious, china-shop choreography, as though she might break herself through gesture alone. She never spoke to me. If I closed my eyes, I was alone.

Afterward, she was inverted and slung from the doorway in the conception harness, her face plump and flushed as she dangled there, waiting to seed. I was shuttled from the house and fed a hot plate of brown cakes: pounded, sizzled, and salted. Vials of water were stashed in my behavior kit, and I drank them without reading their labels, gargling first, swallowing short and hard, spitting just a trace of water back into the grass around me, as instructed.

As I waited on the lawn to be let back into the house—a clear flag hoisted over the fainting ledge was the signal, indicating the young Silentist's removal from the harness—I could not help looking past the learning pond and across the field at the solitary figure of Larry the Punisher, holding the glinting speech tube over my father's receptacle. Larry never seemed to tire out there. Even from a distance, his figure proposed direct menace toward my father, his head enveloped in the vacuum speech hoof, his arms keeled back as though he were readying himself to dive headlong into the earth. There was no clear route to where Larry stood—no road or path that I knew of— and I wondered how Mother and Dark had placed him there, whether through an airdrop, digging, or catapult, or if Larry was an overland expert in the style of an early Thompson, who could assert his own person into those distant areas that harbored prisoners such as one's father.

On those afternoons when a seizure of darkness blotted my presence in the field and rendered our Ohio locale dim and prematurely brown in the air, birds sliding fatly overhead on solid slicks of wind, I whispered from my grassy hideout in Larry's direction, hoping that some of my sound might gain the speech tube and make its way down to the man-sized room that held my father, though I knew that to add more words into his sealed container would only hasten the bursting that awaited him, dosing him ever faster with a language weapon that promised a slow, sure rupture of his body. I whispered hard until my face hurt, risking even the all-vowel words that had the longest-range acoustics and the most father-specific messages I knew of, but Larry never flinched. If he heard me, his body did not show it. My message went softly soundless in the space between us, drowned out in the field beyond, and I lay breathless and spent in the grass.

Mother and Jane Dark did not instruct me or much explain my role as sire, other than to direct that I hold the bottom pose with my young visitors and strike an arch during my release, a gesture Dark referred to as "the send." I was always to send high, releasing on an upstroke. If I sent low on a downstroke, leaking would occur and the send might fail to gift. I was to breathe throughout the duration of my send. Failure to aspirate created a weak send. Too much aspiration, as with Rapid Family Breathing, created a send deemed too watery by Dark, who had tested my send water, produced under differing controls, including sends coaxed from me while my mouth was stuffed with cloth, sends I gave off while wearing the life helmet, or sends I made under the special wind of a foreign language whispered at me by Bob Riddle. I was not to send without a Silentist present, or a Listening Group citizen, or a motion-reduction committee, who would receive and bottle my sends for dispensation throughout the Ohio or Little England districts, where Silentists were seeking to breed. If I ignored this rule and sent alone, that was called a "blown send," but I counted many of them regardless, because I had found a soft old suede glove of my father's, which gentled my stiffly burdensome nighttime error into easy, sweet sends often just before I fell asleep, sometimes in less than twenty handshakes. Mother found me once in the morning with the glove still wrinkled over my hand, as though I had the big loose skin of an animal hanging from me. She sat down and wrote a note of warning against the solo send, her brightly scratching pencil the only sound in my room. "We depend on you. If you require to send again before sleep, please raise your readiness flag and a visitor will make a withdrawal. I'll trust you to discard the prisoner's glove on your own." After handing me the note, she administered eye contact, squaring herself off and sitting erect, staring at me hard until I looked away. Her stare had a kind of wind in it that pushed my face around; I could never eye it directly. This was her typical preface to a dose of wind-box emotion removal she had scheduled, and I braced myself by twining tightly in the sheets, to keep from accidentally striking her if I thrashed too hard. She positioned her hands in front of my face and commenced a knot-tying gesture just inches from my mouth, scratching at the air as if it were a hard surface, a kind of semaphore she performed from memory, and soon whatever I had been feeling or thinking was just quietly scraped away: a gray vacuumed container ballooning inside me as my heart started to zero down and forget its special complaint. I felt scrubbed clean and plain, siphoned off, leaked. Not content. Not angry. Not happy. Not tired. A minus condition. There would be no thrashing this time.

As she stood up to leave, my face twitched with the slightest traces of wind, aftergusts her fingers left lasting only as long as her body did in my room. I tried to breathe, and I managed to get some air into my chest, but the air felt thin and watery and false sloshing around inside me, and I preferred to keep as much of it as I could on the outside of my person.

Every time I was summoned to sire, I wanted to handle the heads of the girls, to grip their faces, clutch their brittle tied-back hair, clasp their necks. If the girls rocked over me too fast, or swooned away from my grasp, or otherwise struck damsel postures that rendered their heads slippery or elusive while we coupled, my send became equally elusive, I grew distracted, and my error might wilt, or, worse, wooden too much to ever yield a send. My hands sought to press on the girls' faces as they rose and fell over me, my fingers pushing their mouths into the shapes of speech, which the girls sometimes vigorously resisted, as their muscles had settled so long against the strain of spoken language that their faces would pull or seize if summoned for talk.

Because this obstructed our transaction, and often dislodged a chew ball a girl might be harboring in her stubbornly shut mouth, Jane Dark issued a directive that a clay head be fabricated to incite my arousal, to ensure I might nurse a prop regardless of the damsel style my Silentist partner had adopted.

Before long, a large and heavy head was brought to me, forged of the kind of clay that is dense and skinlike, the way a real head should be, and I never worked without it. It was kept in a mesh pouch on my father's door. During my spare hours at night, I etched a shallow beard onto the long face of the bust, and I fancied it to resemble a great man whose name escaped me, too unpronounceable and beautiful, a name burning hot in my mouth the more I forgot it, someone who had led his people to a promising hill in a country very much like our own, though lower to the sea, with smaller and softer shelters, with food that hovered at eye level, where the water was the same temperature as people's faces and the wind was thick and pale like glue, slow enough to climb onto and ride over the low grasses. He was my comfort, this man who did not require a body to be important to someone. I held him to my chest or just above my face, so that I could look into the flat mud of his eyes while my body below me went to work for other purposes.

If the session was at the noon hour, Dark often rehearsed her emotion-removal behavior stances near the window while the girl pursued her draw. I cried out loud on those days, without emotion, weeping after my send, shouting throughout the engagement, barking as many consonant sounds as I could until the room filled with a chunky vocal percussion.

As she rehearsed, Dark's shadow blotted the wall in pristine geometries, smooth globs of shade too perfect-looking to fall from a real person. Her movements seemed designed precisely to give off unexampled shadows, as if her goal were to be an originator of a new kind of shade. If ever she was practicing at the window while I was enjoined with a girl Silentist bobbing steadily above me, I could look only at Dark's shadow as she threaded air with her fingers, kneeling or crouching, balancing on a knee and a wrist, a cheek and a heel, images that nearly told whole stories to me, but not quite, leaving me feeling itchy and short of breath. Bolts of cloth were fed through the rafters to absorb the excess consonant sounds I let into the room, and some girls quietly hyperventilated while we coupled, inhaling the extra noise I spilled over our bodies. The cloth work must have been that of Bob Riddle, a man whose every move seemed to silence the world around him, because the more I thundered out plosives and hard sounds of the throat, the less I could even hear myself, so strategic was his laying of the listening fabric, which soon formed a clear lattice over the bed and began to quiver just slightly as it absorbed my commotion, rendering a finely deaf room. And if there was something to our practice that Dark found correctable, she would stand in the muted air at the bed and guide the two of us, her hands as rough as oven mitts. Sometimes I deliberately flurried my stroke or counterthrusted and withheld my send by dislodging my error from my mate, just to draw Dark away from the window and over to the bed, where her hands would soon apply an adjustment and I could feel her labored breath against my face, hotly spiced with the scent of a special water she brewed for herself alone.

My diet at the time was mostly a witness water brewed from persons watching me copulate. At night, I was administered a sleeping water that went down thickly and made me dizzy under my blankets. It dried on my chin and I felt bearded as I slept, my face tight and bristly, but I did manage to sleep anyway, in hard gray stretches of time. On days off, I drank children's coffee and ate a great share of potatoes in the darkened meal room. I drank copiously and peed often, with the sense that I surrendered far more fluid than I took in. Brown cakes were only available after a send, which meant that on some days I fed on water, seeds, and nuts alone. There was beef on rainy days, but it hardly rained, and the beef, when it came, was solid and dry as a button.

The witness water was simple to make. An observation deck installed onto the northern wall of my father's room allowed girls in line for the service to see what was in store for them, to study the copulative transaction and jot down any questions they might have, to mime their fucking on a small hobbyhorse that had been stationed there. I heard nothing from the spectators as I labored at my sends, but I knew that the bit of mottled wall that separated us was thin and clear enough to let them see me. As they watched and waited, small vials of water lining the shelf of the booth stored the girls' impressions and became resonant with the spectacle of intercourse. This was witness water: water stationed in the vicinity of persons witnessing something grand, a lucky water, a learning water, a real behavior liquid. I was to drink the liquid that had been near my own copulation. It would keep me primed to continue; it would make me fertile. My sends would be teeming and lumpen, rich with children. Sacks of new water filled the room by my father's bed, awaiting injection into the small cartridges that were portable for Silentist outings and stillness retreats. The water tasted like nothing at all, and I was not allowed to salt it or dip my leftover cakes. After a dosing, I would think I had swallowed my share, when more would dribble from my mouth and down my shirt, warm and sweet as perspiration. If Mother was present, she would rub the spill into my chest and fix me another glass, hovering her hands over my face in a potentially soothing gesture, bowing her head toward mine as if she might embrace me, then miming a series of quick dry kisses in the windless vicinity of my cheeks, chewing at the air, her mouth pinched into a pale wrinkle, no color to her face at all. If I moved to meet her, to feel solid contact with her kiss, she shied just away from my gesture, always keeping a smooth column of air between us, a no man's land that neither of us could enter.

By the new year, none of the girls were speaking and nearly all of them were listless as pillows out in the yard. It was difficult to deliver the send when the girls were in such a way. They would gradually cease bobbing and seem near to a kind of disturbed sleep above me, drowsily teetering in place, heavily slack in their faces. It was a time of much policing in the copulation room, for no one was participating with vigor, and there had so far been zero conceptions from all of our labor. No pregnant Silentists. No gifts to the Silentist lineage. No new quiet girls with pure blood and a head start toward stillness. I was so far not a father. The bulletin board in the mudroom featured a small neat zero if I ever checked it.

Jane Dark and Bob worked together, providing spots and corrections, performing stand-in maneuvers, shadow demonstrations, silently critiquing their sluggish young Silentists, who often failed to stand freely and had to be propped in place or strung up in harnesses. The stillness rehearsals of the girls had made them unfit for simple movement. They were too good at doing nothing, and now their bodies were soft and puddly, with skin spilled slowly over the air, a bright red mouth bubbling somewhere in it, some dull hair dashed over the top. Often I was summoned to work through cloth, at night, without the girls' entire knowledge, a spotter providing bump assistance behind me at my hips in case I tired and experienced a send delay.

Sometimes I was permitted to play a tape of favorite conversations to help myself achieve sends. The *Lectures of the Presidents,* with its hiss and static, its Old English mannerisms and extended weeping, its fitful animal cries in the distance, was soothing enough to deliver me through such moments, allowing me to ignore the oceanic, unbodylike forms of the girls I was paired with, and proceed as usual until I had sent through. With the tape on, and the old clay head in my arms, I could close my eyes and enter that special time when those historic leaders shouted their hearts out to the world, lecturing feverishly until their bodies collapsed and they died. I could imagine myself near the burnished podium while the greatness of their words crackled in the air above me. My picture of that time was so vivid that if I held my breath and strained, I could even see all of the helmeted children standing obediently in the audience, holding their slender candles that drooped under their hot breath, their faces awestruck with the words of their leaders. Such moments beckoned even the most elusive of sends from my person, and I could host several visitors in a single afternoon. But the tapes grew warped with use, and since Bob required a vowel enhancer and a consonant muffler on the tape player to keep our atmosphere silent, soon it was merely a slow, droning hum I heard from the speakers, no different than someone's father might make if he was bound and gagged beneath the bed, crying for help in his breathy, underwater way.

By this time, Mother was fully quiet and roved mainly at night on a motion sled pulled along by a team of girls. She required the convenience of various locations to accomplish the last of her silencing, but she could not spare physical movement from her ever-diminishing motion quota to get anywhere, thus her need for the girls and the sled, which took a great deal of engineering work on the part of Bob Riddle to operate quietly. He fitted the joineries of the sled with a soft and durable Hushing Bread that muffled the squeaks of the gears, moistening the shrill squeal of the runners on our cement floor. The sled disgorged a share of fine crumbs in its wake that were swept by a Silentist in my mother's retinue. She wore the crumbs in short sacks around her hips and they were later recycled with a new batch of bread, a secondary set of loaves that had yet greater silencing powers. If Mother lumbered at all in the mornings, she was crackery in appearance and fully breakable. She seemed to be stalking an animal in slow, instructional frames of action, and could not help but mock the simplest of motion technologies, like walking, which she performed more sarcastically than anyone I've ever seen.

Straitjackets lined the halls. Many of the girls, deemed barren or sufficiently advanced in their practice, had entered the final stages of their promise of stillness. They would no longer be submitted to intercourse. Their days obtaining sends had ended. They were ready to take a paralysis on our property and sign their promises against motion. Stillness rehearsals took place in the sheds along the water by the fainting tank. A bright red bolt shot across the door indicated a stillness procedure in session. Girls applied the straitjackets: full-bodied canvas buntings equipped with a rip cord leading up to their mouths. When they approached a self-induced full stillness, usually after three days, they yanked the cords with their teeth, and their bodies were released in a heap on the dirt floor. It took them a week to move fluidly again, even with the assistance of a masseuse, and their faces were long and dry with pale brown welts, as if their elective paralysis had set off a decay in their skin. After a stillness rehearsal, the girls cautiously rehydrated with quiet water and examined the film footage of their mistakes, how they flinched and fidgeted, what broke them back into motion.

By late March I lost the potent fire that caused my error to wooden. A small, strong girl came to my room, eyed me fiercely, then sat over my legs, but I had nothing but smush for her. I had given them all so many sends, but it didn't seem to matter in my current condition. After waiting for me to finish fumbling with it, she laughed silently in my face, pulled up her pants, and strode from the room. My error rested cold and wet on my belly.

Dark peered in afterward and queried me. She wore a burlap glove and ran some tests, her body stiff and formal as she busied about the copulation room. "Cough," she said.

"Hold your breath." She meant for me to do both at once, and I tried, despite the pain it caused my back, the sense that my bowels might release. With my breath held, I managed only the driest rasp in my chest, made even harder with the grip Dark held on my exposed bottom. "You're not trying," she said, tightening her hand, pressing her other palm over my mouth. I summoned a cough again, higher-pitched, my face sealed up from air, and something gave way in my back, a scurrying that was sweet for just a moment before darkening under my skin, stiffness creeping over my torso as if it had been injected there.

Dark's hand gave up my bottom and she stood, ignoring my grimace. My error was cold as a worm. She moved to the window and bent into a deep maneuver that involved a pretense of a search for something on her own person. Her arms were hard to follow. She patted at herself while lunging, creating a complication of limbs I could not decode or even watch without feeling nauseous. The shadow she made on the wall looked like a house, slowly dismantling. It seemed to have very little to do with her body—the lines were too delicate and numerous, the shadow too intricate, but it moved exactly as her limbs did, swelling and shrinking as she changed her position in front of the window. With so many sacks of water in the room, I guessed she was creating some special sauce for me, gesturing intricately in front of it, seeking a witness water of an entirely different design. But I was not thirsty. I had drunk enough water. There had to be a period when people could ignore water for a time and let themselves run dry. I shrank further and rolled off the bed to get dressed.

At first I wanted to think that the cold weather had put my

blood on slow, since I was shriveled and blue in my skin, too tired even to monitor what kinds of water they gave me at night. But later that day Dark returned with a heater that she placed beneath my father's bed until I was inflamed and sweaty, engorged with blood everywhere but at my cold hips. It did not help. I wrestled with an error that felt like nothing more than a finger without its bone.

Mother sprayed a fine mist of behavior water at me that night. She sat listlessly in her sled and seemed barely capable of squeezing the bulb of the atomizer. Much of the water blew back over her shrunken, unmuscled body, and she shivered as it settled on her. She fumbled with the bulb, her mouth wet and slack and colorless. The water was an extraction of pure copulation-witnessing liquid, and it had a fine, clear glimmer, like very thin honey. I soaked in it, as instructed, and sipped down several jars more, but my error simply retreated further and failed to respond. With a clipped series of gasping breaths, my mother signaled to the girls, who quietly pulled her from the room in her sled. She left no notes for me.

Alone, I paced the room for some time, slapping lightly at my unresponsive error, before I finally took the clay head from the door and lay on my back in the darkness, holding it to my chest, stroking the stiff beard, my hips exposed and cooling yet more in the sexless room. I was not sure what was happening inside my person, but something thick held me high in my chest, surging surely and slowly in my blood. I did not know it as a certainty, but it corresponded to what I had read of the sensation referred to in the *Behavior Bible* as "relief." An actual feeling, one of the restricted ones, one my body had been sutured against forever ago. An immunization I had taken under the great helmet when I was a child. I could not remember its use, its purpose, the particular demographic of those persons who practiced it. There was a special history of relief, I was sure; a pattern one could study, a population of relieved people who had much to say about it, techniques to describe, precautions to issue. There were tall-standing adults in northern towns who fiended for relief, scheming through sleepless nights to get it from one another, letting their own blood out into small jars until the feeling washed over them. If it was true, it would be happening to me despite my diet, despite the fainting course I had undergone that fall, despite the high, scribbling wind-box treatments my mother had filtered over my face almost weekly to cure me of emotions, cleanse me of the feeling virus, shed me of every loudness in my heart. But despite the precautions of my mother and her team and their highly complex safeguarding work against sensations relating to the world of emotions, I may very well have slipped past their doctoring, their shields. There was a flaw to the wall they had built, and it seemed connected to my wilted error. Quite possibly I felt something that night, even if I did not know its real name and did not know how to feel it, what to do once the feeling started, where to put it, or what exactly it wanted from me. Something was happening that I knew should be kept secret.

I closed the door of my father's room and did my best to breathe.

On those increasingly frequent mornings when I could not send, Dark and Mother retreated to the stillness shed, where they took fainting spells for each other and labored their mouths over the chew stand, which left me free to walk the field and get a closer look at Larry the Punisher. His presence never wavered, but during some sundowns Larry took a seat on what must have been a stool or stone placed above my father's container. He removed the speech hoof from his face, placed his head in his hands, and heaved. I could not ascribe an action such as weeping to him. Possibly he was taking the deep and complicated breaths required of a full-time language punisher, a weapon-breathing technique he administered to restore his full word power to himself. Darkness fell too soon for me to tell how long these rests of his took, whether he was down for the night, or only an hour, but I observed many of them, and at such times could picture my small father pacing the length of his cell, peering up at the ceiling at the sudden silence, wondering what had happened to the stream of hard language funneling down at him. I was curious if his body was yet buckling under the words being fed into his room, and if these reprieves allowed him to breathe easier for a time, or took some strain off of his bones and head. Possibly his body had failed already, brought to a final pressure by the Attack Sentences that Larry was orally injecting into the room through the speech hoof. In that case, Larry was shouting out there at a dead man, who could be killed no more. His work was finished and he could drop the hoof and throw down a tombstone already, mark the site, sing a quiet all-vowel song for the life my father had lost. Even a prisoner deserves a funeral. All that language was being wasted. Larry was shooting bullets into a corpse. He might as well have come back to the house, or gone wherever a person like Larry went, and left my father's body alone.

I did not send up a flare. I did not speak. I did not approach Larry's position far out in the field and wrestle the Punisher down, steal his key, and rescue my father.

Instead, I rolled onto my stomach from my distant zone and thought that if I was entrenched in the grass directly above my father's receptacle, I could burrow my arm into the soil and grab his scraggly head with my hand as he stalked around, pull my father by his hair up against the roof of his cell, even if he kicked and writhed against my grasp like a man being hanged, wriggle him through the hole my arm had made, and release him back above ground, even if the constriction of the narrow hole killed him on the way out, even if he was already dead by the time I had rescued him, even if his body had been fully and terminally language-shot, so that it was bones and skin and hair only, a torso rent by words, mutilated in its pressure box by the choicest and hardest and cruelest sentences, which had been composed precisely to dismantle a father's body, to leave just a face and teeth as soft as bread. Even if all of these things were true, I could burrow him out of there and lie in the grass with whatever was left of my father's body. The scraps, the bits, the broken head, a shoe. Have a companion night out under the flat black sky, beneath the radar of winds and birds, just out of range of the girls in the listening hole, too low for Dark and her shadow-location technique, too quiet even for Riddle to hear us. In a region my mother's new sled could not obtain. Me and my father out in the field.

The New Female Head

A FEMALE HEAD LIBERATION SYSTEM (FLUSH) follows the theory that experiences, which may or may not cause an emotional response in a woman (we may never know), filter first through her head.

If the head's hollow space (chub) is filled with materials like cloth, an ice Thompson, wood, or behavior putty (also known as action butter), then less life can enter and, perhaps, fewer emotions will result.

This approach works best with cultures that believe the "person" operates from somewhere inside the head, that the head is the command center of the body, driving it in and out of the home, forward and away from various "people," and toward attractive bodies of water where the woman might replenish herself for later conflicts. In a survey of the female population of the Ohio countryside, a three-quarter majority of women touched their faces and eyes when asked which part of their body contained their "self." The remainder touched their hands, hips, bellies, or bottoms, while a small percentage of women touched other people or animals or simply grabbed the air. For better or worse, the head, for most women, is still an obvious indicator that a person is in the room.

The emotion-removal strategy, then, is to cut off stubborn feelings before they start, by walling up the head's unused space with various fillers and props and glues, to catch, block, or deflect the incoming behavior stuffs onto another person or animal. A careful woman can then use her head as a ricochet ball or "grief mirror" and bounce her feelings onto her family, to slow their progress or surge them with a debilitating emotion.

If a woman can reduce her chub to 1 percent of total head volume, chances are that very little of what happens to her—including the death of a child, the loss of a friend, or gaining an important promotion at work, just to cite a few contemporary examples—will have any effect on how she feels. She will be immune to emotion-causing events, better prepared to launch into a new and distinctly female space. She may later choose to empty or even increase her chub area, but only after she has zeroed her heart.

A Caution When Using Props in the Chub
When filled with fabric, wood, or an ice Thompson, a woman's chub danger is deactivated, but the resulting fabric waste, spoiled wood, or mouth water, all known as "heart chaff"—marinated in the overflow of feelings, and bearing the impress of a woman's mouth and every consonant-bearing word (crack) she has ever uttered—becomes hazardous and should be disposed of properly.

What Do I Do with Heart Chaff When I Am Done with It?
Landfills for heart chaff have turned into a kind of American behavior graveyard. Female looters, scavengers, and behavior instructors have stormed these chaff sites and walked off with barrels of used fabric and chewed wood, still soaked with the behavior juices of the former owners, a dumping site of Identity Medicine that is far too dangerous to inexperienced women. This kind of American behavior transfer—chaotic and outside the eye of the government—will most certainly lead to diluted strains of female identities and an absolute detour from name-based behavior ventures and Null Heart attainment strategies. To prevent collective behavior sharing, several safer methods are available for the disposal of chaff, or any cloth that has been deeply chewed by a woman. These methods include:

1. Weaving children's clothing from heart chaff and donating it to the misbehaved young people of this country, who might wear the new suits of clothing—often brown and roughly textured, like a woven graham cracker—and thus relearn some of the basic life actions.
2. Creating flags and flying them outside of women's houses to advertise the favored behaviors and feelings of the family within.
3. Building elaborate behavior-free shade zones in open fields by creating tents from the chaff that will shelter those women who no longer know what behavior they would like to exhibit. Resting in the shade of a behavior tent allows women to comfortably plan their next move without the embarrassing pressure of sunlight, widely

thought to exacerbate behavior on the surface of the world. Important behavior tends to occur in darkness, or not at all.

What If It's Too Late?

Let's say a woman's chub is not properly stuffed, a worst-case scenario, where her head has defaulted to its status as a prop-free object in the American landscape. Then key life events invade her head and riot into important feelings, a mess of attachments, hopes, and regrets. Is there a way to manipulate the female head after these emotions have begun, a sort of morning-after treatment when the woman is on the verge of feeling something?

Absolutely.

Because residue of an emotion apparently does remain in the mouth (except in deaf individuals of America, whose emotional activity is stored on their skin, in the form of behavior oil), coats the tongue, and probably does something quite unbecoming to the teeth and lips and gums, it can still be absorbed by the appropriate rag—that is, cloth that has "heard" the secret speech of the woman in question.

The Thought Rag

When women in the American territory speak careful sentences into a handkerchief, they are creating, whether they know so or not, an important item called "a thought rag." Once confided to, the cloth becomes a listening towel, or "priest," regularly privileged to whatever a woman chooses to say. The cloth may be tied smartly to a skirt or blouse, or used as a scarf or bandit rag; sometimes an adventurous woman employs it as a wind sock (if she needs to handicap her actions, lest her skills intimidate her acquaintances). Regardless of how it is worn, it stores a tonal material in its surface and can begin to contain what is crucial of the women who use it—a record of those female citizens who feel comfortable storing their basic life messages (I'm sorry, Go away, It hurts, I'll take it) in a portable medium such as a swatch of stylish fabric. Even a carpet sample can be used, although rough cloth can chafe the face and mouth of the woman, leading to facial weaknesses, like weeping.

Everything a woman feels or suspects is to be confided to the thought rag, as with a diary. This takes all the noise of the "inner life," the so-called dialogue with oneself formerly thought to be so crucial to sophisticated living (though primarily a device of "men" to justify and complicate long periods of inarticulate confusion), and exports it to an object that can fit smartly into a woman's handbag. It is a far safer way to store the fundamentals of a female identity, and the head becomes devalued since it no longer stores a woman's mystery.

These swatches of cloth can be exchanged between people when a shortcut to intimacy is desired. Indeed cloth-swapping salons and thought-rag sharing allow a woman to keep abreast of the personalities of her friends and acquaintances without the troubling ambiguity of speech and imprecise self-representation. A thought rag cannot lie; it won't fail to impart the key data of the person who has used it. If I were to meet you, I would rather spend several hours sniffing and mouthing your thought rag than with you personally. You would no doubt try to impress me or somehow manipulate my experience of your person, concealing your fears and doubts, foregrounding some unbearable fiction of what a person should be. Your thought rag would give me the whole story in an hour or so and I could then decide if a meeting between us would be worthwhile.

Yet swap meets of this kind are also how a thought rag can become lost or stolen, and a woman's identity can be "chewed" by another woman. In such cases, a thought rag can be assigned a password, generally keyed in with a gnashing sequence of the teeth.

Is the Head Itself Still Essential?

At the time of this writing, the head probably cannot be omitted from the person pursuing the female life project. Radical antiemotionalists have attempted a head-free trajectory in the world, yet these pioneers, while laudably testing the limits of the female life project, have unfortunately defaulted their ability to report on the effects of their experiment. They have gone too far from our world for us to understand them. Perhaps one day this approach will seem heroic, yet a woman without an operative head is still unable to signal her former world; to observers, she is nearly similar to a deceased person—her skin is cold, and she does not respond when prodded or splashed with water.

But a compromise is available for those women looking to limit the role of their heads in their behavioral and identity-development enterprises. This compromise involves cold-treating the female head with an item known as the Zero Hood, or facial cloak, form-fitted to a woman like a ski mask and meant to flash-freeze her face and skull. The head can withstand short periods of deep freezing several times per day, as long as the Thawing Sock is applied directly to the woman in time to prevent memory loss. Husbands and brothers are the best assistants for this sort of technique. Machinery should not be operated by a woman using the Zero Hood, nor should she go near children or animals.

Lastly, if each woman of America carved a wooden version of her own head (rook) and polished it with a personalized cloth, speaking kind words to the head (as one would talk to a plant), whispering in its ears, kissing the mouth, and grooming and oiling its surface, a woman might discover a person-shifting relationship with herself in which her own head becomes less important to her life, a prop to decorate, certainly, but not to be deployed much beyond that. This wooden head could be placed in rooms where a woman's presence was desired, a kind of surrogate ambassador for her life, during those many moments that would otherwise exhaust or disgust her real head, the one that still suffers from responses and upsetting reactions to the world at large. I am not embarrassed to admit that I see a world one day where many beautiful wooden heads fill a room, while the people these heads represent are able to rest alone in their cabins and still accrue important experiences with other people.

What About the Nostrils and the Ears?

These important orifices are still a mystery; nearly nothing certain is known about the nostrils or the ears. The more we speak about these enigmatic absences, the further away we seem from any real understanding. It is an unusual bafflement to the American science of the head, and I have always been encouraged by my teachers and surrogate mothers to simply pause in silence if ever questioned about the true nature of these elusive areas. I stand with my head bowed and allow full reverence to accrue until my questioner understands how sacred is the lack of information about these parts of the head.

The Myth of Suffocation

A mouth filled with a bolus of wood or a full pound of linen does not necessarily mean the woman will not be able to breathe, only that her body, once blocked at the mouth and nose (and thus enabled elsewhere), will revert to its internal oxygen stores and alternative "breathing" methods, such as the "emotion furnace," in which the body essentially burns its own anxiety for fuel when the mouth is clogged, rendering an emotion-free American citizen. After the initial panic of suffocation is surpassed, a feeling of relaxation and ease sets in, and a woman will notice her feelings rapidly quitting her body, bringing much-deserved silence into her heart.

Furniture for the Head

A chew stand should be established in the home. In time, it will become the essential emotion-quieting furniture for women. It can be a coat rack with a wooden ball at the level of a woman's mouth, for her to approach and chew, several times a day, to leech herself of grief and rage. This cools the murdering impulse that sometimes occurs in a well-populated American shelter.

Alternatively from the chew stand, a wooden chew ball can be affixed to a doorway or window frame, so long as a woman can approach and fit her mouth over it without cutting or cracking her lips; it must not be too big or too small, nor should it be pliable enough for her teeth to diminish its size. If the height of the chew ball is incorrect, a woman will cramp at the neck or calves.

The chew stand creates an elegant opportunity for American women to pause in their daily lives within their homes and fill the largest chub of their heads with a finely polished wooden sphere. In this instance, wood is considered to be a meat, yet a durably inedible meat, a kind of pure protein that renews itself. A chew session can last for half an hour. If the sphere is cleaned between uses, many women can enjoy the chew stand, although identity compromises (relationships) may result, since wood can only leech so much heart static from the emotion banks of a female citizen and will start to "feed back," flooding a woman's mouth with the identity water of the last woman to chew on the ball.

Women of financial means, who are prepared to spend more money on their own behavior alterations, might consider posting an armed guard at the chew stand to prevent men and other fetishists from chewing and sniffing their wooden ball. A well-used wooden ball begins to smell sweet. Sometimes men will lie in wait, or they will carve tiny versions of their own heads and replace the balls with these. Many women will chew up a man's head this way.

What Is Behavior Putty?
The residue a person leaves behind after performing certain tasks, like chopping wood, speaking to a crowd, buying a sack of nuts, or lunging through a Silence Hoop in an Ohio wheat field, can be collected in a jar, labeled according to the action that produced it, and then used as a topical ointment to prevent that action in others. It might technically be considered as a jelly history of life.

I am not sure why it is sometimes called "action butter," but the term offends me and I would like to see its use forbidden.

Butter is one of the most important items the world has seen, and to equate it with behavior is to deny its potency not only as a key form of animal water but as probably the most reliable soundproofing rub the American body can withstand without seriously harming the skin. Butter also lubricates a woman's body to maneuver through American weather with a minimum of friction. She becomes a secret person within the wind. Without butter, a woman might be seen everywhere, pushed and pulled every which way. She would too easily be a target, plainly revealed and vulnerable to every kind of sighting.

Women's Pantomime

THE FIRST OBSTACLE TO EXCELLENCE in women's pantomime is the surplus of small bones in the face, feet, hands, and body. True mime is best done from a near-boneless approach, when the flesh can "rubber-dog" various facial and postural styles. The kind of mime most often produced by men with a full set of bones (a stack) is stiff and lumbering, hardly believable as an imitation of real behavior. There are simply too many nonpliable bones in the body to allow for the covert shapes and postures that lead to useful emotion purges. A woman who tries to mime away her excess emotions while operating with a full stack of bones will find little success. Only a "short stack" mime style can effectively contribute to the quiet heart.

The chief way to determine the gratuitous bone content in the female head (shabble) is to tap its surface with a facial mallet over an extended period of a month or more, using a mallet style more like *worrying* than actual smashing. Worrying the same area of the head with the mallet will eventually break down the excess bone matter, much of which is at the back or crown of the head, and it will pass naturally from the body, through the tears or saliva or sweat. Any bones that can be shed this way are not important to the life of the body, but are a disposable shell that simply needs to be cracked free and passed.

A small-boned woman who can add at least seven pounds of pure facial weight, without increasing mass to the rest of her body, would not need to remove any bones from her head. The added flesh would be sufficient for even the most elastic of mimes, including the pancake and the puddle styles. The best way to fatten the face through spot gaining is probably to drink cream at the rate of a gallon a day. Another option is a fat transfer from a richer area of the body, like the thighs or hips. With the fat transfer, the fat is brusquely massaged up the torso, into the head, then tied off with a tourniquet about the neck until the fat catches and takes root in the cheeks and around the eyes.

Barring these difficult methods, which only work with the small women, every woman can safely achieve a short stack of bone content by sacrificing several pounds of thin bones in the hands and feet, two rib bones, some gratuitous material on and near the spine (flak), the kneecaps, and parts of both shoulder blades. The bones, once broken, dislodged, and pulverized, can most safely leave the body from a bone exit zone introduced near the sternum.

Other bone removals are riskier, but the rewards of mime adaptability are all the greater. Removing a portion of the jawbone allows a woman to perform the hammerhead mime, good for quieting nearly all of the emotions, but envy in particular. Boneless hands can be pulled into excellent shadow shapes and silhouettes, enabling the chicken and the waterfall. The armless mimes of Geraldine include the weather vane and the elephant, not to mention the sleeveless John Henry. Since all teeth but the front two are disposable, their removal allows for inner-mouth and foreign-language mimes, which are widely effective with conditions of empathy and awe.

Given this rather dire recommendation for such an excess of self-surgery, it should be cheering to hear that the disposable bones, once broken and dislodged, don't always have to be removed from the body; they can be migrated under the skin to the belly area, or pushed around into the excess flesh of the buttocks, where they will keep for months, provided the buttocks are regularly massaged and soaked in water. Restoring the bones to their original locations is easy; they can be shuttled through the skin until they arrive at the home area, then a body vise, a so-called Restorer, might be layered underneath a denim bodysuit for a week or so, until the bones have rooted again and returned to their former function.

What Do I Do with the Bones After I Remove Them?

If enough hardened bone remains after removal, a behavior whistle, or body flute, should be carved. Music played through an instrument derived from a woman's own body will tend to calm her feelings, pacify the various rages of the day, and offer a sense of collapsed time, which aids in decreasing attachments for persons or things. The songs from the body flute may also be effective in halting the motion of others, or causing them to sleep or cry or harm themselves, depending on the tune that's played.

Animal Mimes

It is only natural that miming an animal (slumming) would produce an internal animal state of reduced feelings. Most persons, including women, regularly slum an animal without knowing they are doing so. A basic zoological catalog of actions, such as the *Behavior Bible,* can be followed by the miming woman (the quiet Gladys) looking to cool down the intensity of her feelings, and these animal actions can more or less be subtly integrated into daily life, appended to the so-called human behavior a woman exhibits, so that basic tasks like walking, swimming, reading, and speaking can be augmented with various animal behaviors: stamping the feet, mewling, scratching, bucking, kicking, lumbering, hissing, skulking in the grass. It will be for the individual woman to determine which animals offer the behavior models she most needs to eliminate or conceal. There are so many animals in the world now, and the history of behavior has become so vast, that a woman should have no trouble finding a creature that corresponds to her emotion surplus (fiend quotient), but the search for an appropriate animal should very likely begin on the American farm. My animal-mime practice, when it was required of me, centered on a creature known as the horse. The horse postures, stances, and attitudes I pursued—the trot, gallop, canter, feeding from a bag, shaking my "mane," rearing up with my "hooves" when I was introduced to people—including an intricate program of neighing, whinnying, and snorting, which I deployed orally at every opportunity, until I had successfully and legibly integrated bursts of these noises into my everyday speech so that I appeared merely to be loudly clearing my throat—these horse intrusions required so much attention from me that the result, at the end of the day, was inevitably to leech me of every active feeling I was aware of and thus cleanse my rioting heart down to the simplest, pumping thing. Indeed perhaps the chief effect of miming an animal is a kind of deep exhaustion not possible otherwise.

My earliest memories of my father involve his dog mimes, then later a wolf act that became indistinguishable from his real behavior, an addition to his fatherhood that kept him out-of-doors, knocking about in the yard, hard to please. During his dog phase, in the mornings at our Ohio home, he prowled outside my bedroom door and growled and scratched and barked, sending up moans and howls and threatening sounds, sometimes gnashing his teeth as though he were tearing at a piece of meat. He often pretended he was eating me. If I went to the door, still cautious and confused from sleep, to determine what was the ruckus, I'd only hear him scamper away and discover in his place nothing but scratch marks and slobber and a strange odor, along with a hard, dark nugget of waste. Upon my return to bed, he'd be back at it, barking his hard, father's bark and pawing at my door, throwing himself into it, whining.

My mother's animal of choice appeared to be a creature I could only fathom to be another woman, very much older, probably her own mother, who was stooped and sad and sometimes aimless. It was a quiet mime, with only the subtlest style, the most refined behavioral imitation I've ever observed, entailing long days of stillness by the window, elegant use of her hands to hide her face, and a deep expulsion of sighs that bordered on language but lacked, always, the requisite shape of the mouth to carve the air into words.

Is There Anything I Should Not Pretend to Do?
Miming an emotion is the most dangerous gestural pretense, for obvious reasons. If an emotional condition is unintentionally mimed, such as weeping, laughing, wincing in fright,

doubting—even when done as a joke, as though to suggest, Wouldn't it be funny if I actually felt something?—the only real antidote can be an extended performance of the nothing mime, a stationary pose held outdoors for a full day, which requires a woman to do exactly nothing until the mimed emotions begin to subside. The danger of a mimed emotion is that there is very little difference, if any, between pretending to feel something and actually feeling it; in some cases, the pretense is even stronger, the imitation cuts deeper and lasts longer. Thus the nothing mime, conducted in any weather and deployed with the use of a full-body mood mitten, which registers a woman's emotional activity on its surface, is prescribed.

The Thrust Mime

The gestures of intercourse (stitching), when undertaken without another body or prop, are useful in purging feelings of confusion and doubt. If I do not believe I can accomplish a task, performing the thrust mime, an extended stitch and volley, tends to erase my doubt and send me back into my life with renewed commitment. My common stitch occurs with a wide stance against a waist-high table, one arm crossed behind my back for balance, the other leaning on the table (military push-up–style). On the count of three, I begin to thrust, a slow pace at first, smooth and solid, with a striding tilt to my hips, as though I were probing a stiff pudding. I drive deep with arched back and clenched buttocks. At the full-thrust position, I "flurry" with short, fast strokes, then pull back and "go long," slowing the thrust almost to a stop and drawing all the way back (the seesaw); intermittently, I withdraw and hold a long pause, then nozzle at the threshold, which involves rising up and down on my toes (also called Peeking in the Window), before returning to the basic thrust and flurry rhythm, the parry, the dodge, the throw. This style also works over a staircase, though both arms are used for support (the civilian). When practiced against a wall, a shoulder can be relied on for pivoting, with both arms clasped behind the back (the gentleman). People will naturally have to discover an authentic thrust mime for themselves, based upon the primary gesture that brings about release. They may also employ a bump coach, if their budget permits it. If the act of thrusting is not the chief sexual gesture, then the mime should be changed accordingly. Knitting and pecking are other useful intercourse paradigms. I have seen women perform the elegant fade-away jumper mime, the elaborate sauté, the arched mime of hula hoop, and the rise and shine, a somberly grave sexual style that always saddens me, and I suspect these actions were based on sexual experiences, given the gentle facial tremors I observed and the strained gestures of concentration. There are probably thousands of different ways to mime human intercourse—to stitch the air with one's hips—not to mention the many animal styles that also have their uses, yet a woman should not be discouraged if her intercourse mode is different or unusual to witness, if it requires a complicated and new physical presentation that might frighten other people who could mistake her stitch for a seizure or rough sleeping. A deceitful, conservative stitch is helpful to no one, nor will anyone be fooled. More and more women, during moments of doubt and confusion, will be pausing in their daily affairs to mime briefly a personalized moment of intercourse, however strenuous and interruptive it might first seem, and thus recover their courage to move about in the world.

The Good-bye Mime

The good-bye mime is probably the most therapeutic behavioral imitation available, yet the very notion of therapy involves a promise of relief, which itself is one of the more stubborn American feelings, and not to be succumbed to, so this form of fake behavior should be treated carefully. If too much comfort is derived from performing the good-bye mime, it should be discontinued. In short, the good-bye mime involves constructing nonflesh enemies who can be "killed" through mime weaponry, strangling, drowning, and other means decided by the woman "waving" good-bye. The kill function, as a general behavior in this world, is not available to very many persons without legal consequence, yet a certain *love reduction* can probably only be accomplished through the mimed slaughter of persons orbiting the woman's life, especially those doing so to an excessive degree, the fathers, the brothers, the so-called lovers, the strangers. A nonflesh duplicate of these enemies, or mannequin equivalents, can be aggressively mistreated by a woman at will—stabbed, shot, punched, and pummeled—and the result is an outrush of attachment sensations (friendliness), which can be the most resistant to emotion flushing. The good-bye mime should be executed at a private kill site, where vocalizations may be freely released and a wide cache of weaponry is available. A woman should kill her father, brothers, friends, and relevant strangers in this way whenever the *trap of devotion* begins to feel too real.

In turn, the suicide mime (carpenter), done when a woman's personal shame volume (psv) has become overly loud in her body and threatens to produce undesirable acts of contrition and apology, is a useful self-killing mime that, if performed frequently enough, can accelerate the zero heart attempt. In my experience, the suicide mime must be arpeggiated to work well: I must rapidly fake many suicides, through gunshot, hanging, and knife wounds, miming the actual death moment each time. Women might prefer to "Shakespeare" the death moment and draw it out over a full day, while others may find that "cartooning" it is more effective for shame reduction.

Equipment

The very notion of women's pantomime is to conduct a life without things, so equipment itself becomes a paradox, and, with one or two exceptions, should be refused in favor of a pure mime life that could occur anywhere in the world without alteration. Although some women prefer to wear the full-body mood mitten and the empathic storm sock throughout their daily activities, I view this choice of attire as an arrogant display of reduced emotions, somewhat too preening and boastful, insulting to those persons who still are addicted to expression and emoting.

Yet one important device is indispensable to the frontier of women's mime, and that is the body-correction full-length glass, the Translator, which serves as a window in front of the miming woman and distorts her actions in various ways: It makes her seem more friendly, it "males" her or "ages" her, it delays her gestures and plays them back later, for behavior festivals, and it creates a mirror template of refined women's actions, for her to model her body after when she is practicing her behaviors.

Would It Hurt If You Mimed Your Father?

Miming a member of one's own family (ambush) can create an interesting behavior minus that can nearly last forever, particularly if the family can work as a team to mime one another's behavior (a figure eight), doing so in real time throughout their daily lives, swapping roles during those hard hours between sleep sessions. A camouflage mime occurs when several family members suddenly mime a single person (bull's-eye), as when parents mime their son, for instance, and do not relent or admit that they are doing so; this is also called "overmiming," or "love," and can cause a very durable behavior minus in the boy whose behavior is being imitated, particularly if he goes by the name Ben Marcus. The overmime absolves the boy from being himself, given that his behavior is so well covered in the actions of others. He can watch his parents acting as he would, imitating him, until his head and heart become so quiet and small that quite possibly no one in the world can see him, and he can make his exit from all visible life without report.

Dates

1852

WOMEN IN MIDDLE DENVER seize celebration rights to the annual Festival of Stillness, previously observed and dominated by men. They travel in groups to mountainsides and forests outside of town, drink girls' water, attire themselves in stiff sheets of weighted cotton, and seek a final, frozen posture, hoping apparently that the mountain weather will fossilize their bodies into a "one true pose," to represent them for all time. Their bodies are displayed in a traveling exhibit called "Women's Behavior Statues," and teenage girls are asked to study and rehearse the more basic positions. The slogan "Action is harm" is coined that year and the Festival of Stillness becomes a dominant women's holiday.

1934

Early Ohio weather is first captured and preserved, then played back later through a simple AM radio. These radios can be taken on picnics to the lake, for customized weather and simple wind performances, benefiting the other families parked there to eat sandwiches and cast pebbles into the water. If several families stationed on blankets along the shore play their radios in a simulcast, calibrating the tilt of their antennas to focus their broadcast just over the water, the sky appears stronger, the children's words are clearly enunciated, and the currents in the water ripple more realistically. Every family has a favorite weather style, and a radio that will play it back for them. Sometimes it sounds like the shortest words of the American language, in particular the first names that are used to summon people up from sleep, to groom their heads with a softly blowing oil, preparing them to be addressed by the largest person in the house, often the mother or father.

1939

Long Island physician Valerie James, thirty-six, and a sister begin a practice devoted to what they call "Women's Fuel." She has studied anatomy with a local medical group for three years but is otherwise untrained. Before she develops her notorious line of medical drinks for women, the James Liquids, or Water for Girls (1955), she and her sister will attempt several techniques of altering the disposition of women: the water chair, bolted to the floor of a medicinal pool, which holds a woman underwater until her lungs give out and "expel from the body all toxicity"; a sleep sock slung over the doorway, that women might sleep "in the fashion that they stand"; high volumes of wind shot at a woman's body to "massage the senses"; and endurance speaking (or language fasting), in which the woman speaks rapidly until collapse, to "deeply fatigue the head and free it of language pollutants." Only the sleep sock, which enforces a female sleeping posture, will prove to have lasting credibility, although the language fast is adopted and modified by Sernier, who requires his students to undergo it before attending his lectures.

1966

A clear sock is devised by the body-sleeve specialist Ryman that will protect a woman's head from men's language, the so-called weapon of the mouth. The sock also works to block the entrance of television and radio transmissions, certain man-made aromas, and men's wind. Because breathing is difficult when wearing the Ryman sock, fainting often results, and it is through this accident that the Listening Group discovers what it will term the "revelatory power of willful fainting," and adopts the belief that regular drops in consciousness allow women to hear something deeply secret in the air. The Ryman sock will be fitted posthumously to the heads of dead Silentists, to aid their attainment of a possible women's afterlife.

1968

The first official version of the "Promise of Stillness," a vow against motion, appears in January in Albany. The document argues that motion and speech disturb the atmosphere and must cease before a "world storm" is generated that could destroy America. The Women's Congress, which fled to Albany from Boston in December, has commissioned local radio announcer Katherine Livingston, twenty-six, to risk her job by reading the document on the airwaves while, throughout the country, the signatories take their final positions, mostly in their homes, before ceasing all motion and speech. Emily

Walker, the most vocal of those women to take the promise of stillness, issues a statement, declaring, "If I die, it will not be of hunger. I am not hungry or thirsty. I refuse the false promise of motion. I stop." She dies in six days after shedding a brittle layer of skin, the Walker Pelt, which hangs still in a New Jersey home. Her cause of death is listed as starvation. In the years to follow, Walker Pelts will be marketed to families as small body rugs to be thrown over children, either to immobilize them or to reduce the falsity of their motion.

1971

Silentists attack Fort Blessing, Texas, July 19 and kill five members of the Listening Group before kidnapping seventeen-year-old Caroline Ann Parker. She will live peacefully with the Silentists for four years (until "rescued" against her will by the Texas Mounted Police), marry Quiet Boy Bob Riddle, and stage spectacular, noiseless demonstrations in the Texas desert. As a professional Listener, Parker will be employed by the Silentists to discover an American territory with broad parameters of silence, a region where silence will not only be possible but required. They will settle in Ohio.

1972

Martha Ferris develops Women's Sign Language and tours the country, demonstrating the technique at schools and churches, proposing a women's bilinguality that will not only allow for private utterances but possibly enable new forms of thought not available under current systems of grammar and syntax. Her younger sister, Katherine Ferris-Watley, has pierced her own eardrums during a local show of silence and refuses to learn American Sign Language, keeping her hands swaddled in cloth, and often "signing in tongues," a form of gibberish sign language thought to have religious significance. It is from Katherine's blunt and frustrated semaphore that Sign Language for Large Hands emerges, a system of forceful prop-aided sign language meant to be read from a great distance, utilized by Silentists who have injured or burned their own hands in protest but who still must enact a basic language. Women's Sign Language will be rejected by the deaf communities, since much of it requires that the hands of a woman be pinned against her hips while she jumps and spins in the air, actions that deaf women, with their compromised sense of balance, are unable to perform safely. The Listening Group, seeking further difference from the Silentists, will establish a new but troubled relationship with the deaf communities, believing that their skin is receiving the sound that their heads cannot, leading to the Deaf Pelt Thefts of 1974, an action of massive scalping and skin theft against deaf persons.

1980
Sernier kills Burke and is acquitted. He says that if he had it to do over again, he would have killed Burke more slowly. He wishes he could "continue killing Burke." Burke's family silently walks through their Akron neighborhood while people jeer at them with the chant "Burke is dead." Burke's scholarly works are no longer widely stocked in bookstores. The grammatical tense that Burke has proposed—Burke—is rejected by the Omaha Language Council on the grounds that it renders improbable things too plausible, because it "makes no linguistic distinction between what can and cannot hap-

pen." In August, Sernier's students attack seven men and women who were said to have been students of Burke, forcing them into a Thompson Box, a clear cell with a speech tube attached, where the input of language disrupts the rhythm of their bodies, leading to seizures and ultimate physical arrest. Sernier applauds his students in an editorial, asking readers not to forget that he killed Burke. He promises that the word "Burke" will hereafter create a "lasting wound to the skin." Jane Dark promptly adopts the word as her first language weapon. She demonstrates that by shouting "Burke!" at a small dog, it will not be able to walk and will soon collapse with fatigue.

Names

[Erin]

THE ERIN IS A KEY GIRL in many American houses. It is often misnamed Julie, Joanne, or Samantha, and sometimes it is clothed as a man. As a man, it is still beautiful, although less visible, and prone to lose color during sleep. It makes love and has slender legs, while persons that see it are eager to palm the spot where the woman parts would be, to sweep and pan their hands over the heat of the man that is hiding her. Persons pry a finger into its mouth and feel weak and sweet in the legs, deriving pleasure through this gateway into Erin, breaking through the husk of a man's body into an inner body named Erin, sometimes breaking past that also to touch at the smooth core and stain their hands on it. There are text versions of Erin, as well. Reading them is similar to seeing Erin. It takes a day to read the full version of Erin, and the process is exhausting. The text cannot be memorized and sometimes the ending comes abruptly and frightens the reader. The first lusciously bright pile of Erin that the others feed from is located in Denver and kept warm by a man named Largeant. It must be swallowed quickly or it will cut and wound the mouth.

> *Statistics for Erin:* My sister refused all clothing but an old beige throw rug. She crawled around under the rug, mostly at night. No real language was exhibited, though she made rudimentary attempts at Burke. She seemed concerned to exhibit clean geometries with her body beneath the rug: circles, triangles, squares. We could not get her to wear a sleep sock. If she fainted, she did so without our knowledge.

[Tina]

The Tina will die. It will emerge in Chicago and reside in chipped white houses of wood and warped glass. It will die quietly. When it does not emerge in Chicago, there will be something uncertain and weak to its shape, a rough tongue, and hair that a father has unjustly handled. It will die on a Tuesday and the hands will go blue. There is promise to the newer Tina shape. It is blackened through ancestral practice, but it can be watery in color. There is a milky storm nearby this Tina figure, and girl versions often dive into the heart of the wind for cleansings. Nothing by way of an answer is ever found in it. On its back is a mark, a freckle, a blister, a scar.

> *Statistics for Tina:* My sister walked upright and spoke basic English. Her face approximated gestures of "happiness." Her nocturnal actions were mostly low-level postures of sleep. Excellent wind resistance. She showed confusion when we stopped calling her Tina. She had already decorated some of her belongings with this name.

[Patricia]

It isn't the most willing shape to swim or lunge or use force to motion over the road. The body prefers the easiness of a chair and a stick to point at what it likes. It is most fully in the Patricia style in the evenings, with brittle hairings and admirable mouth power. They have a Patricia everywhere now, sometimes many. There is no conflict in an abundance of it, which can be considered the chief difficulty. There are many and yet it seems as though there are none. It will be born in America and will exist most successfully as a child. Often the Patricia system lives well into the last posture before demise, beyond the view of childhood. Age falls all over it and makes it walk down into the ground and sleep as though it lived in a grave. It calls out from its grave phone, but the ringing sounds only like a sleeping dog and is ignored. It is then allowed to witness itself as an earlier thing, a thing best seen young. The older Patricia fights off the young girl Patricia. It will kill it down again and again, achieving nothing, but killing it nevertheless, creating space for something else that is new and wildly bodied. The young Patricia eats a large bowl of corn for pleasure. It weeps at the sight of water.

> *Statistics for Patricia:* My sister was mostly pliant as Patricia. She willingly posed in several behavior statues for my mother. No resistance to the Brown Hat, which allowed her to converse fluently with several of my mother's assistants. They spoke a language that sounded like slow laughter.

[Carla]

There are fabrications that go forth under the Carla tag. They are smallish and brown-hued. There is an actual Carla at a school, and it will learn to beat away the fake occasions of its own number. It will see one coming up the road, one little brown Carla, with fingers like American bread and a hairdo cut right out of the afternoon. The real Carla circles the false object and places fire on its living parts. Many times, an American fire contains glittered fragments of a combusted Carla. There are fires in Ohio and girls are leading their dead parts into them. Every morning in every city young women are seen chancing a look back down the road. Sometimes a sluggish fat-skinned fake is sulking back there, waiting to take over and fail in Carla's place. When the Carla makes comfort with boys under trees and farther out on the landscape, there is an apology to the movement of its hands. It touches a boldly upright kid's penis and then palms the dust, the soot, the soil, feeling for the tremor of legs approaching.

Statistics for Carla: A name regularly used on my sister. She showed frequent bloating and could not fit into the sleep sock. A Ryman sock was used with much discomfort. Her evening mimes were striking as Carla. Often she could calm the entire household.

[Nancy]

I saw one at a bed. It kneeled; it leaned. There was hair and a body and no such thing as weather, no window broken onto a wall, nor water rushing behind us, or a road to remind me I could leave. Something like this is waiting to happen for everyone. A room somewhere sweetened with a Nancy system. You can approach it and examine its teeth. They are the color of an old house and have chewed their way through something—a trap, a net, a man's hand. I let my arms operate like they did when I was a little boy. I "held" it. It did not bite; it did not speak. I stumbled. It gestured for me to rest. The Nancy shape cannot be detached from the woman it stands for. It can be released, to drag a bed—from a rope looped over its hips—into the city, putting to sleep the visitors that approach it and speaking to them certain facts, certain secrets as they dream, until they can rise from the sheets and move away from it into the distance, toward an area lacking all Nancy, dull and shoe-colored and simple, an American city with other kinds of "people," and life beyond restriction.

> *Statistics for Nancy:* No skin was shed after my sister used this name. My father repeatedly scoured her body with the pelt brush, to no avail. The only language she exhibited was to say "Nancy" until she collapsed with fatigue. A highly harmful name. Possibly a harmful word. None of us enjoyed calling her this.

[Julie]

There is probably no real Julie.

[Linda]

From 1984 until the winter of 1987, an absence of significant registered Lindas spurred a glut of naming activity in that category by parents eager to generate unique-seeming figures into the American landscape and thus receive credit for an original product, the Linda. The resulting children are emerging mostly out of Virginia, with a possible leader, or group of leaders, working through Richmond. Examples have been seen in the West—small and shockingly white, with delicate eyes—

but they have been in poor health and have not lasted. Weather cuts them down and hides their lives until it is too late, and they die. Sometimes rain is blamed. Sometimes nothing but wind. The adult community—too old to register their names and therefore unable to receive the benefits of official status—has nevertheless been supportive of the surge. The tall and stately Lindas, with plenty of money and a husband, have politely vacated their homes, allowing the new Linda children in for full access to their men, their things, their lives. The older ones enter a sack and wait.

Statistics for Linda: High-level exhaustion during the Linda phase. My sister showed bewilderment and frequently made evasive maneuvers. Quick on her feet and difficult to catch. Often we could not find her. She seemed inclined to play dead. A nonuseful name for her. Highly inaccurate. May have caused permanent damage.

4

Planet Jane Dark

———◆———

Teachings of the Female Jesus

Promise of Stillness

The Fainting Project

Dates

Names

Teachings of the Female Jesus

ONE NIGHT WHEN THE AIR was torn up by papery clouds, and the calendar showed no siring appointments for me to meet, I skipped my evening water dosing and slid back the red bolt on the door of the stillness shed.

I did not often skip my water intake. It was not thirst that set in without it, but wrong thoughts in my head that could not be mastered, and a pulse in my chest that fired too fast and stalled my breathing. It was a disruption that could lead to mistakes: memories, for instance, which could lead to other mistakes, like feelings. This was water that put me to sleep: a long, calm stretch of time to keep me blank until morning. The world speeded up without it. The people in it became blurry. The water was like a blanket inside me that I could crash against.

There were no guards outside the shed to monitor access. It was a night of pure Ohio silence. In daylight I could not go near it without encountering an escort. That night I walked upright and crunched through the grass and no one came near me. It was easy to be anywhere. The women were all sleeping.

A dark brown light stained the inside of the shed. A dirty fog. It smelled like something. The structure was once a barn, a simple wooden box, with wide boards smeared in a honey varnish. Every day I watched the women file in, carrying their stillness equipment. Heads down, serious, hushed. Sometimes a thin coil of smoke arose from a perforation in the roof. Otherwise there was nothing to see or hear from the shed. It was muffled in some deep bunting, as quiet a house as there was on the whole compound. If the women exited, they did so discreetly, at odd hours, without sound.

The air inside felt rumpled, as thick as cloth on my face. I moved into it slowly, squinting into the deep brownness. On the floor, sitting in neat rows like students, were more stillness practitioners than I could count, many rows deep, their bodies receding into the darkness at the back of the room. They were flush to the walls, with hardly a lane left for walking. Several bodies lined the near walls, fastened upright with harnesses, as if they were participating in a carnival ride. There was equipment everywhere: rigging, piles of cloth, chalkboards. Many of the women wore straitjackets, though some were covered in makeshift corsets and capes, draped so deeply in cloth that their bodies were not visible at all. It was difficult to see much. I tried to look at their faces, but they were downturned and some were covered in what seemed like gauze. I waited in the doorway, adjusting my eyes, trying to breathe quietly, shallowly, to keep the odd scent out of my mouth. My entrance did not seem to have disturbed them. It was as if I had walked into a room of the dead.

Out of the silence came short blasts of high pitched breathing, a synchronized hissing that suggested their bodies were connected to some vast engine beneath the floor, firing air through these women as if they were just pipes. Possibly this was a form of unison breathing. Crowds of women breathing in sequence, a political breathing, precisely timed, producing their audible wind, then entering a hard inhale all together, clearing the room of oxygen, stifling anyone not following their calibration. The room felt like a large dry lung.

I stepped in and tried to navigate toward the back. There was hardly room to walk. With my dangling hand, I accidentally touched against some of them. Their bodies were cold and rigid. Their skin had the same clammy density as my old clay head. None of them flinched at the contact. No coughs or groans or shuffled positions. I was possibly one of the temptations they had trained for, a man in their midst, an opposer to challenge their stillness and tempt them back into motion. They were good. I felt thoroughly ignored. The room refused to come alive.

I had read the report on the atmospheres in the shed. As women motioned down, their exhalations thinned out and they needed less oxygen. The air in the shed would go unused, thickening around their bodies. It would be a paralysis air. A straitjacketing air. It could be a bottled stillness. Injected into canisters to quickly rid a room of its motion.

The more of it I breathed, the slower I moved. If it had a taste, I could never describe it, but it made all other air I had ever breathed seem weak, an air that did nothing for a person but dry out his insides, make his whole head brittle and cold, lather him with age. I felt myself filling with a kind of sweet sand that would fill my gaps, coating the hollows inside me until I was solid and heavy and entirely finished as a person.

I am generally no strong advocate of breathing. I do not appreciate the labor behind it, the gruesome inflation of the chest, how it fattens a man's face and advertises his hunger. Something as necessary and regular as breathing should not require such shameful heaving, such greedy shapes of the mouth. There is no civil, polite way to do it without embarrassing oneself. I prefer to hold my breath when I can, to feel warmth spread through my face as my emotional fire stifles inside me without any air to feed it. As much as one inhales even the best of mountain air, the supposedly healthy, rich oxygen of the countryside, every breath produces a small disappointment, fails to soothe one's inner body.

I pushed deeper into the room. It was so quiet I could not hear myself move. In the far corner was a small area free of women, equipped with a blanket and a low ledge of water vials, a case that looked like a behavior kit, and several swatches of rough-textured fabric. A small framed photo of Jane Dark as a teenager was nailed to the wall—a little girl in braids performing a dance for the camera—positioned for a devotee to gaze at as she sought her private paralysis. There was a technology to the area, a sense of expert outfitting, suggesting that if anyone would ever succeed at stillness—even a man who had been told that the project was off-limits to him—he might do it here, in this advanced setting, with perfect conditions.

I took my position on the carpet, lowering down among the women. I wrapped the blanket over my shoulders and braced myself with wedges of carpet. My legs felt wrong beneath me, stiff and aching. I tried to sit upright, but the muscles high in my back burned in such a posture. I scooted into the corner, which held me better, and pulled the blanket over my face, until the wool heated against my mouth and I was breathing into its scratchy surface, fully covered, hidden in the back of the shed.

I waited for the great merit of stillness to hit me, the benefit of my motion camouflage. Much of the literature of stillness posted on the bulletin board was coded just out of my range, either vowelized or rendered in a foreign tongue, too difficult to decipher. To look at it always left me disoriented and tired, knowing less than when I started. I wasn't sure if stillness should make me feel more or less. Huge feelings that racked the body and could never be reported to the outside world other than by a seizure of weeping and wailing; or a clean, quiet heart that shot jets of forgetfulness through the blood, antidotes to complaints, leaving a calm minus in its place.

I waited there under the shroud of blanket, breathing all over myself.

That is all I remember.

I was discovered the next morning by the motion warden. I presume that's who she was. She sprayed men with a terrible device. It lured them into motion, dosed their bodies with frenzy. She kept the shed free of false students, policing the women for weakness in their practices. I do not know how she found me, unless my smell was a trigger, unless they knew I had escaped the house, unless she had seen me enter the shed and was waiting for the precise moment to spray such crazy motion onto me.

I had seen this warden before, training on the compound, but she had never come for a send. We had not coupled. Probably she had failed at silence and was not selected for mating. Too noisy in the mouth. Banging around through her life.

She took her afternoons in the exercise yard, doing face work mostly. Usually she stayed low to the ground, showing a great strength when operating from a crouch. A body not suited to silence. Too powerful to stay quiet. Sometimes she took part in evening helmet burnings, when an edition of silence helmets had expired.

The warden crouched and applied her prod to my legs, a charge so hot and deep that I thought I had wet myself. Her dog hissed at me like a cat, a raggy thing with terrible breath, jumping around me and blasting its awful air into my face.

The sudden daylight in the shed burned my skin. I could not detect that any time at all had passed since I had sat down to try my stillness. It seemed to have been a single moment, but when I attempted to fend off the dog, and could not move, I guessed that the night must have passed, and possibly more time than that, because my limbs felt cemented onto me, my skin a quicksand that could drown me. The stillness I had gained did not want to surrender me, even as the warden's ministrations increased, pumping a heat into me that left me twitching around on the floor, fat and warm in the hands.

Much disturbance commenced at that time in the shed. Once the women abandoned their poses, a full vigilante system was launched, and I came under their methodical, slow siege, more threatening because of how leisurely they approached me. They fell and writhed in the dust as they shouted their all-vowel invective, chanting high-pitched songs full of scolding, angry intonations. The women looked very much at sea, reaching up to me as if I might save them from drowning. The volume in the room had been raised, possibly with the opening of the door or the sudden movement of so many Silentists. My eyes and ears smarted with the brittle sounds, even those my body made as it rubbed against itself, and I felt for the first time the allergic reaction sound could produce after so much silence. It was a sound I could not digest, and my body convulsed to reject it, but it smothered over me in too great a wash. I felt a rash coming up under my skin like a suit of sand.

An alarm rang somewhere. I found a lane free of bodies and took it, forearming past the warden and into the women who had sprung from their straitjackets to grab at me. I was on my feet and powerful and not long for that shed. I muscled myself roughly through the crowd. They were easy to disperse, their bodies hollow and dry. It was like pushing through stalks of wheat. I was afraid they would break when I touched them. They cried out sharp, high notes as they toppled, quivering quickly on the ground, their hands grazing at my legs with no force at all.

Soon I had cleared the last of the women and found the door. Only the sky was above me, the shed a wooden mistake to my rear, a shrill vowel invective still pulsing in the air like the sound of a distant celebration. I ran brokenly, wrongly, until I only heard a faint hissing behind me, as delicate as water, a hissing sound that in the end was just my own legs, pumping hard and fast through the grass, taking me away from there.

Mother did not try to search for me, though I knew she would require an encounter. She might attempt to administer decoy praise, to confuse me, or present affection mimes to ironize my behavior. A silent party might be thrown in my honor, with clear cake and children's coffee. Women hissing at me, swatting the air, charading their pleasure. Possibly a deep behavior massage was forthcoming, strong hands kneading my body with a lesson. There would be a return to some primary learning water in my daily dosing. I might receive a wind-box application, or she might require me to sit in front of the behavior television. Unless, that is, consequences themselves had been phased out of the wide-scale behavior reduction at work on the compound, in which case my trespass in the stillness shed would go unremarked, even on the bulletin board. The event would be silenced. No reports would be issued, my schedule would not change, and the behavior that met me would be as steady as ever. I would be left to devise my own reaction from the encounter, a private analysis to sort out a moral from my breach of the stillness shed, my disregard for trespassing rules I knew well. Or I could choose to disregard it myself, to store the event nowhere, to mime my indifference until my indifference toward the event became real.

I was hidden deep in the yellow field when I saw my mother's dim form in front of the house. She swayed slightly on her feet and waited for me. I saw no sled, no assistants, no fainting equipment. My mother was operating solo. A person appeared to have collapsed near her feet. I felt so little already that I was too tired to feel less.

I waited until a bluish darkness filtered over the field. It seemed possible that my mother might exhaust herself out there and lose her purpose, forget why she was standing outside, or, at the least, suffer enough fatigue to diminish the strength of her treatment. We could wait each other out, compete toward apathy. See who cared more. Or less.

I killed the afternoon by moving my limbs, massaging the

blood back, though even my fingers were stiff. All motion seemed wrong and foreign. My body refused it. The hard air that had settled over me in the shed had left me capable of only the smallest gestures, useless movements that could not gain me food or make me understood to others. If I tried to speak, I could not move. If I moved, I could not speak or breathe. If I stopped thinking, my limbs twitched and the stiffness would subside, with patches of warmth spreading in my thighs. A certain coordination had been compromised. I tried not to think. If an enterprising animal had found me, it could have had its way with me and encountered very little defense at all.

My mother was stationed on the walkway when I finally pulled myself home. I needed water. The evening was too dark for eye contact between us, and she had spent her quota on me days ago. She stood stiffly as I advanced, tilting her head toward me as if she were blind, as if she might hear everything about my approach that she needed to know. I circled her and tried to keep walking toward the house, quiet in my step, but she raised her hand, jerked it up, and held it aloft. A gesture to stop. Her back was to me, but her head was cocked expectantly. There was no use in me going anywhere.

The behavior flash cards were revealed as I sat in the gravel of the walkway, the evening air thin and sharp around us. Mother's headlamp provided the light. She mounted the cards on the frame and then retreated slightly to assist her presentation with a languorous wind-box application, shifts of the air that deepened my concentration and made my head feel clear and open. I was not concerned about striking anyone. My body still felt too heavy to use.

These cards were new; I had not seen them before. Each one showed a family scene. The characters were rendered in our own likeness: my mother, my father, and me. A fourth character had been blotted out: possibly a dog, possibly a girl. The cards were drawn as precisely as photographs, suggesting the pictures had been copied from life, but the settings behind the characters had not been filled in. Their actions were suspended in gray space.

The first card showed Mother and Father swinging their boy between them, none of them smiling. In the second card, the boy was afloat and alone, possibly assisted aloft. The third card showed a close-up of the boy's mouth, void of teeth, a red gummy mess. The fourth card was blank, or speckled with dust, or depicting an empty sky. The father's back was turned in the fifth card. He was alone and walking away. The boy was sprawled against his legs in the sixth; flung toward the legs, probably, or kicked away. Then the father appeared in a series of cards that showed his shadow to be more ample than he was, a shadow that began to consume him, oversized, a swollen cloud. The boy and his mother were drawing the shadow around the father in the set of cards after that, even while the father seemed to protest, his arms raised, his hands curled into fists. The mother and boy were using brushes or pouring cans of dark liquid around him as the father's body grew smaller and his shadow blackened over him. In one card, the shadow was pouring directly from the boy's mouth.

We were up to card twenty. My mother used flat hands to stroke the air as she continued her wind-box application. In the next card, the boy received a shock if he tried to enter the father's shadow. Cards showed him being flung back as if from a force field, sparks roving over his body. He could not pierce it, though he made several running starts, even as he was held on a leash by his mother, who was leaning away with the strain. A blotted figure was already resident inside the shadow, in a wagon pulled by the father. The figure seemed immune to the father's shadow, the wagon slightly aglow. In the next few cards, the shadow and the father became one blobby item, and the blob began to recede, until the father was a small black point, no wagon in sight, and the boy and his mother were left alone. The boy's leash formed a tightrope between him and his mother, and small girls walked the length of it, an empty speech bubble hovering over them. The cards closed in on the girls, who were walking along with big smiles. The boy and his mother were too big to be seen clearly in these cards; they were mostly vague shapes in the background. In the next set of cards, the boy searched through a patch of grass for something, poking his fingers into soil, and finally came up with a small wagon, too small to contain anybody, though he tried fitting himself into it. He then tried to pull the wagon, but there were no wheels on it. He showed it to his mother, but she had her head turned.

In the last set of cards, the mother was building what appeared at first to be a house. Her son stood near her but couldn't help because his hands had been erased. He tried to nudge supplies toward his mother with his head, but she didn't seem to want his help. He became smaller as the cards progressed, losing length in his arms, and the mother's construction project grew larger, surrounding her, until it extended naturally from her massive body and began to feature an engine. The boy rested on his back near the exhaust of the engine. He had no arms. The mother was hardly recognizable for the structure that surrounded her: a large, motor-powered house. The last card showed a thin line of colorless fire. No characters were drawn on the card.

My mother dismantled the rack, tucked away the cards, and then stooped to her feet to gather something from the crumple of cloth. The body on the ground was lifeless and too heavy-looking for her to lift as easily as she did, and when I saw its face to be my own, I recognized it as the mannequin that she had built some time ago—a hollowed-out version of me she could demonstrate behavior on. A procedure had been ordered, and she was following Dark's suggestion. Build a dummy of your boy. Use his own hair for the head. I had hardly seen this mannequin. For some reason, it was mostly kept from me. It was a fair likeness, and it showed me to be in good health. It was interesting to see a copy of myself so slack in the body, so pliant, as if I were watching myself sleep.

She dragged the mannequin up on her lap and began a series of hugging gestures against it. She cradled the head in her arms. She kissed its cheeks. The doll was limp as she held it, but she smothered it all over with nuzzlings. She tried to tickle it. She pressed its head into her bosom. Her face was plastered in a smile, stretched so wide it could have been a grimace of pain. She gazed up at the stars, posing her face in various masks of contentment. My mother could certainly look pleasant. She wanted me to see this. There was a lesson here somewhere. The two of them cuddled there in a picture of affection as her lamp burned on and the night grew later.

I watched her loving the doll. She did it well. She had an accurate and complex style of affection. I could easily believe she was feeling love for it. I sat perfectly still in the warmth from the two of them. A photograph of this scene would have convinced anyone. It would have been proof that I had been held, doted on, cuddled, nuzzled, kept warm, and kissed and kissed and kissed. I would like to have copies of such photographs. They would prove interesting and useful for later study. For later regard. It would be good to have evidence of the endearments my mother and I have exchanged.

A month later my sends had yielded zero gifts, an entire winter of wasted mating. My sends were no more than vapor, leaks down other people's legs. In the end, I had sent nowhere. There would be no purebred Silentists, no girls of the new water, no prodigies of stillness born without a bias toward motion, an allergy to sound. No children at the compound at all.

I walked down on the lawn and saw those remaining Silentists, who had yet to undertake their promise of stillness, standing in a circle around the burning conception harness.

Their communication was reduced to a rough hand grammar that looked like a stylized midwestern fighting style. It was performed without flinching, yet consisted of considerable gestures of rearing back, hands ferreted up, retracted punches, ducking and weaving heads. These were pre-stillness women, purging their last spastic actions.

Here they all were, facing one another, showing much gesture of warfare as the harness burned. Some made as if they were squeezing a small animal in their fingers, tearing it apart. Their heads were placid while their hands contorted, their faces erased of expression. At certain intervals in the gesturing, their mouths pitched down jets of wind into their hands and they appeared to be warming themselves like travelers around a fire.

All the staff was on hand, though I did not see Mr. Riddle, the silencing man. A quick check behind me revealed Larry's dim form at work in the field as always, barking hard at the hole that held my father.

Mother and Jane Dark took turns kneeling behind the girls to spot their gestures: guide their hands and correct their motion, apply paddles to their limbs, a short stick to the small of the back, fine jets of water onto the face.

The door to the stillness shed was open and a great noise of hosing could be heard within, the sound of fast water striking something soft and loose, like skin. Many of the women carried packs.

I had not known them to gather at once in this way, to put their bodies in view, to be such plain targets in the daytime. Something busy was afoot, but as I stepped among them their gestures quickly subsided, my motion poisoning the air and killing their own. The women powered down as if my presence had tripped a plug on their bodies, and soon no one was moving but me. It was a field of statues, though their hair still frittered in the low morning wind, and a new scent swirled about the area, the smell of paralysis.

One of the frozen women was my mother. Her body, such as it barely was, had curled around a small cardboard box. She was just another Silentist now, who could not abide being seen, who would not move if a man was watching. Her face relaxed as I approached her. It was spongy and showed no recognition. She was styling herself for me to see her. It seemed to take great effort, but her mouth moved in purses and puckers, a face not practiced at speech seizing now under its strains. She was making the musclings of language, but there was no sound. It looked as though she would eat the space between us. If this was what it took for my mother to talk, to make a piece of loud wind that I might use—in order to know her, or myself, or my purpose—I did not care to see it. I sat with her there until her face fell calm and she was no more than a mannequin of my mother. True to life, perhaps, and accurately rendered, yet wooden to the core. The work of a carpenter, at the most. The work of a person-builder. A very certain kind of no one. A body you could sit next to all afternoon and, with the right kind of concentration, start to forget.

Inside the box, which slipped easily from my mother's hands, sat a helmet as soft and colorless as a man's deflated face. Its perfect oval shape was what I had always hoped my head might look like. I had not realized a helmet could be as clear as water, could make my face feel so small and safe—a tiny, plain face that would seem far away to anyone who looked at it. A helmet to frame me into the distance, so I might look as though I had yet to arrive.

A note in my mother's hand was taped to its slightly hairy top, where the skin was pink and sticky. "Put this on," the note said. "You're going to need it. We will not see you again." I could not look at any of the Silentists. I knew it would shame them to be seen. I did not want to damage anyone's chances, to cause more feelings than I needed to. With a lowered gaze, I picked up the helmet, which proved heavy and sourly scented of meat, strapped it on, and rose slowly to my feet. My head felt older and more familiar, as if something had been missing from it before.

I had vials of water in my bag and many small sacks

of seeds, and I began slowly to make a distance from the house, walking delicately under my own head, listening for my thoughts, waiting for the sound of them to blast back on.

Looking back, I saw the closed door of the stillness shed, the red bolt blazing firmly in place. The women were gone. A motion-free area had been achieved. It took me turning my back, and then they were gone. The shed was full. My own head was finally a finished part of my body. I would not need to worry about it again. The moment called for a dash of new water to be donated, and I spilled it out on the dirt at my feet, where it did not seep in, where it merely puddled on the soil, shimmering a bit in the late-afternoon sun until I stepped on it firmly, squarely, pushing it as deeply as I could into the earth.

I noted the Punisher's position on the horizon. He could have been a fake man, a statue, a mannequin. Too far away for me to tell. Men that far away are as good as dead. It was best that the punishment was happening behind me. Fathers are always punished in the distance. He did not move and nothing near him did either, suggesting his entire location was constructed of color and light alone, with not one single beating heart in it, no real skin, nothing that could actually die. It would not be a place for someone such as myself.

I turned my back on him and walked hard and straight toward the deepest Ohio. My house gained size behind me as I retreated, staining the ground in a clear, thick shadow at my feet, the distant horizon ahead of me breaking into smaller and softer pieces as I approached it. There was nothing to do with my hands then but hold them up and feel around on my face— touch my mouth, my cheeks, my eyes—and maybe discover what, if anything, on that last day at home, I might actually have been conspiring to feel.

Promise of Stillness

LET IT BE RECOGNIZED, under the witness of the all-prevailing female Thompson, that this legal creed against motion bears the authority of a Female Jesus edict, a life law designated by our Lady Freeze, through which a woman of America might prosecute her stoppage of viewable actions, thus joining forces against all that moves, waging war in the name of stillness and silence, creating of her body a fixed landmark, an example of tranquillity, a frozen zone.

By signing this document, I enter into this agreement solely through my own choice, which I assert is mine to dispense. I have not been paid or persuaded to halt the viewable gestures of my body. If I profit from my ensuing stillness, it is from an arrangement of my own, though money I earn while physically still is fully taxable and subject to paralysis funds or other dowries initiated to support motion-free localities and persons residing there or en route to them. I hereby assert that I have not notified any member of the Silentist organization of a financial motive for stillness, a manner that stillness might be construed as employment, labor, or creative endeavor, subject to compensation, or gambled upon by persons betting on the outcome of the promise of stillness.

I agree that none of my garments, while I bear down into stillness, should advertise the interests of a foundation or individual other than myself, and in no way may I be marked, whether through tattoos or scars or text slogans burned into my skin, with symbols that can be construed as citation for anything outside of my own physical interests. Nor may I license my name or likeness for the mercenary aims of those not affiliated with the Silentist organization and its satellite groups. I remain fully accountable for the way my name is used, written, uttered, or in any way referenced by these outsiders.

Should my stillness result in personal debt or bankruptcy, I cannot assign that failure to any motion-prevention society existing now or in the future, and I forfeit any right to seek damages for any change in my wealth status or physical health or emotional condition that results.

Nor will I hold accountable any other woman, or person or animal masquerading as such, for the task which I hereafter set about to accomplish, regardless of the outcome, including the possibility of my disappearance or forceful demise or drowning down a well into the hell pool. That task can be described as the ultimate full stop of every action viewable at a distance of one arm's length or greater, with the exception of fidgets and grimaces, magnified semaphore or rescue gestures, a stoppage also known as the promise of stillness, the life pause, the freeze, the Jane Dark.

The distance of viewable motion detection, if my stillness is ever tested, may not be assisted with motion-detection glasses, gesture goggles, body microscopes, viewfinders, binoculars, a pencil, action-detection wands, stilts, or eyesight-enhancement devices of any sort existing now or yet to be developed, including smart skin, dead face styles, or hand-to-the-earth tremor-sensing techniques of the Indian people and others trained by them. Nor should organic vision in excess of twenty-twenty be the standard eye strength by which the distance is determined, even if the twenty-twenty standard becomes, at some future or other time, an easily surpassed milestone of eyesight, whether through medical or vitamin enhancement, an exercise regimen, nutritional assistance to the head through such devices as the strength sponge, or self-surgery interventions designed to render the seeable far more vivid, applying a close-up filter to that which was technically once far away, a come-hither ointment rubbed on what was once distant, a coil device affixed to objects, pulling them into sight as they are approached or summoned. My body may not be treated with motion-detection jellies, circled by twitch-inducing dogs, smeared with bait to lure me into action, or prodded with an electrical rod.

Should the standard Ohio Motion Detection Device™, as worn by a Jane Dark representative, register natural movement of any sort on my person, or a wobbling palsy arising from my body, as with nervous hands, whether through tethers, leashes, or strings that snap taut if I so much as move, or a sonar device that alerts a Jane Dark representative, who might occupy an observation booth, of motion occurring from my person, this contract shall become void and may not again be undertaken. Nor might any future accidental paralysis of mine, or frozen body condition that I may adopt, whether through enforced stillness, straightjacketing, coffin incarceration, or any other unnamed method of stillness, including my apparent demise, even if it proves a real demise, complete with eulogy, burial, and headstone, or a real demise that lacks these rituals, but still occurs, such as my body flung from a vehicle and come to rest in a ditch, where it is never discovered, but is still technically in a state of demise, be indicative of a successful promise of stillness, but instead shall signify an aberrant or natural pause in my motion akin to a stop-time event in a bird migration, such as birds pausing midair to perform a shadow function on the land below—which in some cases is a system of messaging for those women equipped to read it—or some other unsanctioned event resulting in stillness, such as a personal gridlock, a crisis of motion, or a Syrup Action.

I recognize that stillness occurs by accident all the time, and agree not to confuse these forms of stillness with the stillness I herewith set about to adopt. If I do not know this, I admit that others sufficiently know it, and I grant these others the power of mind over me to know the things that I am not capable of knowing, to adopt the ideas I recognize to be in my best interest, however incapable I might be of holding those ideas on my own, even if I do not consciously agree that the ideas are in my best interest, and even if I actively declare these ideas to be harmful and alarming, or cry out in pain, or beg for help, or disavow the very words of this agreement, or deny signing this agreement, or claim no knowledge of the terms of this agreement.

I further disavow that which randomly or intentionally puts a halt to my body. I disavow bodies that stop through inertia, fatigue, car crashes, and other collisions or unions that bodies make when they persist toward solid objects and become stunned into torpor. I disavow the nonstillness achieved when bodies are acted upon, lunged, hurtled, or thrown into the landmarks of the countryside, including the insertion of bodies into slings attached to the long wooden arms of the great structures known as catapults, which, when activated, hurl forth the contained body into modes of extreme nonstillness, which can apparently result in conditions known as orbit, though often don't, particularly when walls intervene, when trees intervene, or when the body itself windmills and rudders and otherwise drags on the air so much as to render its flight finite, and it crashes down to earth.

I disavow bodies that stop to pleasure sexually against other bodies, even if malicious in intent, even if incapable of pleasure, even if both or all of those bodies fail to gain actual, measurable pleasure from their attempts and instead only become injured, whether they break or bleed or carry the wound within, whether the pleasure attempt results only in sadness, shame and disgrace, irritation, detachment, or nostalgia, whether their bodies fail them or surpass them, whether they merely perform such techniques as cuddling, nuzzling, or cooing. The result of self-styled bodies seeking pleasure against one another is irrelevant to my purposes and I cannot confuse these results with my own goals. Seizures of pleasure that result in spells of rigidity or surges of paralysis, as with orgasm functions that produce even permanent collapse or demise, which I recognize to mainly occur in horses, or suspended postures of sexual rictus of the body that in every viewable way seem to duplicate stillness, are not applicable to elective stillness and cannot be counted among their legal modes.

I disavow bodies that use themselves as restraining devices against other bodies or animals, applying smothering or straitjacketing effects, employing techniques such as the dog pile, the clothesline, the roadblock, all in order to channel a paralysis style, to induce a person or animal, through force, to collaborate on a project of stillness. My stillness, should I achieve it, may not be contingent upon another person or thing. It must be summoned of my own power.

I further understand that this contract against motion does not imply a legal agreement against nutrient input or other body-sustenance strategies, activities falling under the categories of eating or feeding, but not limited to them. Gesture-free nutrition intake is permissible and advisable, whether through intravenous methods or a food-entry system that can be accomplished without the technique of chewing, handling, or in any way moving in relation to the nutrient stuffs. If I hire a male feeder or biscuit person, I acknowledge that I am responsible for any accidental motion that might occur as he moves around my body, deploying the food into my person, inputting it, injecting it, catapulting or throwing or rubbing it in with the poultice, the dinner brush, or the swab. He is permitted to move me while mediating the food into my system, but if I am seen to move toward food or him or anything or anywhere, including but not exclusive to Objects of the Night that roam outside my periphery, this contract is terminated and I might legally be killed by Susan, whom I hereby designate as my executioner should I fail the terms of this agreement. I invite Susan to come and get me. I ask Susan to end my days.

I admit that because all motion can be argued to be a collaboration pursued with another person, object, or wind, there is no time that I am not complicit in my own motion, an accomplice to the crime of nonstillness, and thus already in breach of this contract, producing hard excesses of visible behavior, betraying myself. If convicted, I may be put to sleep with a Thompson Stick and then interred in the Women's Weather

Museum, put on display or exhibited in a show concerned with portraying the various ways women have failed to be still, though I admit that the verb form "to be" cannot precisely be used with regard to the condition of stillness, implying motion as it does, suggesting tremors, frenzy, spasm, activities that are seeable, which by definition are off-limits to me, as all forms of language eventually will be. I authorize in advance the use of my body as a caution against the future errors that girls not even born might be prone to commit, and I hereby license the Silentist organization, and any of its museum affiliates or community centers or shame igloos or apology huts, to apply any curatorial device whatsoever if it is deemed to create an instructional spectacle of my physical error, including, but not limited to, wall mounting, animated installation, taxidermy, hologram, math, flashlight.

Any fasting procedure conducted concurrently with this promise of stillness is an addition I make by my own design. If I fast, I fast under no impression from the Silentist organization, or any similar women's sound-prevention society or listening club, that the abstention of food intake will assist the activity of stillness here proposed. Starvation, should it occur, cannot be linked to the Silentist organization or its affiliates but is entirely the result of my own actions, which have not been influenced by any extant women's group. Nor can I at any time claim or imagine such a connection to exist, either through interpretations of their words or direct citation of such, including, but not limited to, quoting, sampling, footnoting, or applying slogans to my garments. If I starve, it is through my own active avoidance of that which would reverse starvation—namely, food, pellets, cloth, and liquids. I further understand that starvation begins the moment nutrient input or foodstuff acquisition ends, the point at which my mouth cavity lacks population and is fully hollow, save for those objects that have organic residence there, including, but not limited to, the teeth and gums and tongue. A person not eating at this very moment is technically beginning to starve and is thus legally starving, in which case I hereby admit that I am starving right now, already, and thus will have been starving before I signed this document, continuing to starve as I read it, and starving at this very moment, a statement that, when uttered, can never be untrue, which indicates that starvation is a preexisting condition for me and not covered by any grandfather clause endorsed by the Silentist organization. Nor can I assume that to traverse this border of starvation/consumption by sandbagging my head with a lifetime supply of slow-acting food that will drip down my throat for the duration of my alert term as a person is a sanctioned antidote to the problem of terminal hunger, or that there is a sanctioned antidote for the problem of terminal hunger, not to mention a cure. I admit that it is not possible to be in a constant state of eating, or "fugue feeding," because eating interferes with breath. For the purposes of this agreement, I recognize eating and breathing to be in a primary competition with each other to dominate the mouth.

By executing this promise of stillness, I sever all future rights to discuss the results of my actions, whether through interpretation, reflection, public memory, dispute, debate with persons who move, or otherwise. I may not use words or signs of the hand or conduct my face through a gymnastics of code that might present some person or other appropriate receptacle standing opposite me, or outside of the space where I can be said to be standing, even if I am prone on a rug and blinded by pain with a hot poker pressed against my neck, with a coherent notion of what it is like, and has been like, to be, or have been, me. Or, if this pronoun does little to produce the suggestion of my person to the attention of others, *Me,* then whatever word, words, or symbols I use to designate the flesh mistake that covers me, stands for me, actually is me, hosts me, collaborates to materialize my spirit, or leads others to believe that I am being referred to, will indicate my special accident. Doing so shall void me from this agreement and subject me to possible living prison incarceration, hard-motion punishments, or other public demonstrations of discipline to be determined by the Silentist organization or any punishment strategist designated to act on behalf of the Silentist organization, whether publicly or in secret, or otherwise.

I understand that by choosing a personal paralysis zone, or Shush House, I thus designate the spot from which I may not thereafter retire. This spot must therefore be designated with care, and is hereby referred to as the Final Place, though it can also be known as the Den when I am employing covert messages in the presence of motion addicts. Under no circumstances may I infer that there is an ideal Final Place, or any such thing as a recommended area, from which it is thought best to execute the promise of stillness. Such an understanding on my part, as all understandings ultimately are, would be entirely in error and my sole responsibility and surely a potential occasion for future regret, not to mention punishment and breach of contract. Thus I concede that to draw conclusions would be illegally to engage in deduction, which is a process I choose to take on, and fail at, myself, admitting ahead of time that it is my own folly. So-called good-luck nooks and lobbies are only superstitiously termed (as all terming and naming and definining operate superstitiously to outwit silence) and cannot officially be said to impart greater likelihood of success to the woman bearing down upon herself to end all viewable actions. If I choose a Final Place that has already been chosen, or been designated the Den of another woman, be it an igloo or debris hut or woolen tent, I may either seize that place through forcing motion onto the present occupant, tempting her with motion-inducing gestures such as "the crab," "the dash," or "the trot," as well as other taunting semaphores used to regulate the flight of birds, or I may vacate such an arena in favor of an unoccupied zone, though I hereby admit that there is no such thing as an unoccupied zone, that wherever I go, I do damage to what was there, by either killing or displacing it, that my presence encourages something else's absence, that the term "my body" implies no one else's body, that by moving through air and time, I kill what was attempting to rest or habitate or hold steady. I remove that thing from its chosen space and effectively deny its reentry. I act as a warden of a prison in reverse, since wherever I am, no one else can be, so that to execute this agreement is to do a violence, for which I hereby admit my guilt. I admit that even by speaking or shouting or murmuring or babbling or humming, I crowd my personal airspace, and thus someone's potential personal airspace, with code and thus limit the insertion of codes by others, deny their entry, hoard the airways, create a blockade. For this and other crimes of motion, I hereby admit my guilt.

——————————— ——————————

Sign Here   Date

The Fainting Project

FAINTING IS A FORM OF aggressive sleep and Null Heart attainment that has wrongly been seen as a weakness in women. Historical images of the fainting figure in the American landscape, the cinema, and literature seem to imply that the world is too strong to be tolerated, thus the woman swoons to the floor in escape, requiring a comforting rescue and sharp salts to return her to her senses.

On the contrary, fainting will be considered here as a strategic exit from consciousness, a willful blackout approach to the removal or prevention of the major emotions. In the Marcus Family Enterprise, fainting is a heroic pastime toward self-control. By fainting, we insert a curtain against the onslaught of life, and thus structure and silence the awful drama that would otherwise never cease. Fainting, for us, is a way to author our own lives and insert intermissions, the most underrated portion of any entertainment. By not fainting, we surrender our identities to the mundane chaos of time, the relentless needs of so-called people, and the assault of an American wind that possibly only gusts on people who are awake to receive it (sleeping is the only real way to avoid the wind).

Although I am obviously not a member of the 5,000 Falls Club, the elite corps of female behavior changers who have intentionally fainted or blacked out more than five thousand times, I have followed a rigid swoon program since my youth, and still rely on rapid fainting exits from life when I am otherwise too sad to eat my silencing grain, scared of my father's wood shop, or unreasonably pleased when a person touches my head. Fainting, for me, is particularly effective as a killer of guilt and a dread suppressant, though it has unfortunately proved ineffective with shame, a rather more stubborn condition.

The strategic, short blackouts achieved through willful fainting usually offer an easy antidote to the problem of recently acquired feelings. Fainting closes off the offending world; upon resuscitation with salts or girls' water or women's-frequency injections, including radio-wave body baths, most emotions have been reduced appreciably, or at least temporarily forgotten. What this suggests to the Marcus Women's Team and to the Jane Marcus Emotion Prevention Society is that the entire accessible level of feelings—what we think we feel throughout the day, our supposed personalities—is gratuitous and fleeting, given its lack of reoccurrence after fainting and revival. If these were true feelings—indeed, if there were such a thing as true feelings—they would not be so easily removed.

Ways to Faint
The Fainting Chair employs an ejection seat that launches the woman into flight, but not before depriving her of oxygen (snarfing) until dizziness sets in. Usually the Fainting Chair is

of a burled walnut design, outfitted with a Lucite head-gag harness to assist with snarfing before the spring-loaded jettison is triggered. Once the woman's body is fired into the air, the sudden elevation causes a predictable blood shift from her head (diaspora), creating a dry-brain faint that can last until her heart is quiet. The dangers of the Fainting Chair involve unpredictable flight paths, bodies lost in orbit, snuffed ignitions. Nets and crash pads must be judiciously placed throughout the fainting site, and the Smelling Salts Team should be ready to dispense hardened Ohio Salt to the woman's upper lip (winterizing) in the event of a misfire. The fainting site should be high-ceilinged, with unadorned white walls, in order to track the woman's flight into her blackout. To avoid permanent loss of the woman, she should be tethered with a Sleep Leash.

Many women will not have access to professional equipment, but they can easily produce a faint through means other than a special chair. Easiest among these is the spinning, whirling action known as the Candy Cane, or the Barber's Pole. The woman raises her arms to a T shape, then spins in place until the full 360-degree horizon wobbles, tilts, and flattens onto a single plane and a faint ensues. If she is wearing the requisite red ribbon, a lovely spiral is created as she twirls into dizziness, an effect much appreciated by any Blackout Witnesses that may have gathered. A resuscitation team here is not required.

Holding the breath and rising quickly from a regular chair is a cheap, homemade simulation of the ejection seat, and nearly as effective, though flight cannot be achieved. It can be supplemented with a straining action in the face, or a full-body expulsion mime, also known as "bearing down" or "shortstopping," though this straining can burst vessels of blood in the head, which will certainly bring on one or more resistant emotions, usually a pernicious dose of ambivalence.

The False Promise of Animal Fear

A chief use of the wild animal in emotion removal is to create a sense of vulnerability in the woman or girl, to literally spook the liquid from her until she blacks out. An extreme surge of fear can swiftly produce a faint in such persons—the body anticipates the death event and swoons away from the conflict, voiding its consciousness, rather than keeping alert to the last moments of life. Yet the temptation to hire an animal assistant to regularly threaten the woman or girl, often by startling her in her bedroom or bathroom, is misguided and must here be cautioned against, not least because it exploits the animal as a fear chemical. When an emotion-cleansing faint is produced through a surge of fright—that is, the wolf leaps through an open window and corners its prey, baring its bloody teeth and hissing—the fear response is sealed into the fainting state, and thus preserved in the woman or girl beyond any useful duration. Animal fear and other forms of predator anxiety, including the fear of fathers, are the only causes of fainting that could feasibly do more harm than good.

Blanketing the Fainter

Throwing a blanket over a fainted person (Morris) can enhance the emotion flush, or trap the feeling and keep it from escaping. Often an oil-soaked blanket, whose blaze can be easily contained by a Blackout Manager, is best suited for a quick heat extraction of panic and regret, although blanketing a Morris tends to be ineffective against happiness.

What About Dehydration?

A carefully pursued water minus will increase the occurrence of fainting throughout the regular events of a day; it does so by withering the muscle of wakefulness in the head. But dehydration can easily lead to unexpected fainting (visiting the hole), which may be dangerous. A woman or girl should stay close to the emotion-removal site during a water fast, and she should alert her Blackout Manager if she is abstaining from fluids entirely (Moses). The Manager in these cases will most likely affix the woman with a fainting pager or brown beacon, which detects a blackout, or sudden alteration of body position, and emits a shrill siren into the vicinity, bringing on the resuscitation team, who can home in on the noise until they find their downed woman.

The Primary Equipment of Fainting

I am most inclined to wear a stiff, unwashed flesh-colored turtleneck when I practice a fainting style of the antisadness or passion-dampening variety. The turtleneck limits blood flow just enough to deepen the faint, creating feelings of "dry head," or "birch body." While a beige neck corset can also be worn to tourniquet the head—it blends in like a scarf—the danger is that too much blood will be restricted and the faint will deepen and mature into coma. Although coma is interesting, with real potential in future behavior-changing styles, given that it dilutes emotional life in a woman, coma-resuscitation strategies like the Burp and the Bear Hug are still too jarring, tending to result in emotion surges, which lead to dizzying back drafts of envy and regret that create nearly untreatable emotional surpluses, a kind of hysteria of gratitude, elation, and fear.

The Secondary Equipment

The Salt Necklace, padded clothing, a Sleep Leash, a hood, and a helmet are all important accessories to the American Female Fainting Enterprise. A helmet should be worn in general when reading, writing, thinking, or sleeping.

The Salt Necklace enables default self-revival if a Blackout Manager becomes injured or defects to another emotion-removal group during a fainting session. Similar to a string of pearls, the necklace threads together calcified balls of salt, which ride the neck like a choker and sting a woman awake if she passes out too soon.

A Sleep Leash tethers the body to prevent long-distance ejections from the Fainting Chair (home runs). The body is kited to an anchor and snaps back to earth if the launch velocity exceeds the crash recovery quotient, a distance beyond which the body will not survive when it lands.

The padded clothing and helmet allow for hard landings without disrupting the depth of the blackout. Although broken bones can be useful in an emotion-removal program, as demonstrated in the discussion on boneless pantomime, the pain event here is too likely to cause feelings such as grief, fright, and alarm, rather than placate or remove them, which is the goal. The head, in turn, is simply too important at this time to be smashed open.

A hood is merely decorative in the fainting program,

although it nicely conceals the facial contortions of a fainted woman who is struggling against revival. A woman in a hood can make startling gains in this world and elsewhere.

Underwater Fainting

This last-ditch method of fainting is dangerous to attempt alone. At the Marcus Behavior Suppression and Elimination Site, the Fainting Chair was positioned to eject my oxygen-deprived body into the learning-water tank, so my faint occurred in midair and I splashed down in full blackout. The divers on hand fished me out only when my lungs had filled with water, then resuscitated me with a basic bellows maneuver, followed by a salted sock stretched over my head. This is a method requiring teamwork and devotion, yet it adequately flushed the more stubborn strains of envy that often visited my person during childhood, including the envy I felt for myself at happier times. Submerged fainting (wet sleep) should also be undertaken if a so-called loved one dies or leaves without notice, yet women should be alerted that the recovery from this sort of grief is so quick and efficient that the deceased or departed person is sometimes entirely forgotten, leaving merely an empty feeling of contentment where a person once stood. A woman might choose to keep a Person Log in this case, to objectively remind her of the persons who supposedly once mattered to her life.

Dates

1895

CHEMIST EMILY SESSLER, forty-six, heads the first Science Week drive to aid the Vertical Horizon Project, an attempt to extend the typical citizen's field of vision. Sessler's scheme, initially opposed only by preservationists, is to craft a fire that will link the American coasts, the largest fire ever conceived, to burn in a pattern precisely designed to create tunnels of brightness deep into the sky. Sessler maintains that brightening the sky with a systematically designed fire will produce a "Horizon Crane" to yank back the barrier of the horizon, altering religious and scientific notions of the role of the Person in the atmosphere. State governments oppose the science fire, partly because Sessler insists on providing her own technicians to manage the blaze. Her technicians radically lobby for the approval of the fire, and ultimately foil their chances, by setting test flames in the perimeter surrounding Atlanta, creating a vortex of heat-generated darkness in the city itself, causing not only a blackout but a "sound-out." Neighborhoods of Atlanta will be resistant to sound for years afterward, and a localized heat deafness emerges in the South, apparently caused by unnatural exposure to fire.

1935

Burke is born at Akron. Within months, he will use an invented language based on radio static and stuffed-mouth lamentations to control his father and mother like puppets, forcing them to copulate in public and weep openly. The parents will request of the Children's Police that the young Burke's gifts be carefully controlled, but it is suspected that even this utterance of theirs is generated by Burke himself, who sees his parents' bodies as "weapons to be used against the town, satellite forms acting on behalf of my body." Burke's youthful demonstrations will be the first American indication that language, dispensed precisely, can regulate the behavior in a territory. It is eventually suspected that a portion of the town of Akron has been "hushed" by the careful recitation of sentences at the perimeter between Ohio and the world. Although the boy is eventually fitted by authorities in a tight, clear sock, even his restricted pantomimes create a disturbing loss of control in the animals and children in his vicinity.

1954

The American Television Industry attempts to market a Women's Television Set. The unit resembles their standard device, but is designed to receive a special-frequency broadcast from the Women's Storm Needle at Atlanta, where experiments are being conducted in images and sound that only women can perceive (also known as the Female Jesus Frequency). The set receives little attention and will fall into immediate disuse by the few customers it gains, but the Storm Needle continues to transmit an all-vowel female music for five years. This period will prove to be the most crucial in the Silentist movement, allowing Jane Dark and her followers to travel the countryside undetected, camouflaged by the women's tones masking the Midwestern landscape, curling over the territory as, arguably, the lowest and thickest wind ever felt in America.

1955

James Water is cultivated and distributed by the Women's Medical Group. Designed by physician Valerie James, the tonic, comprised of exact water, ostensibly cancels unwanted emotions, as James surmises (prophetically) that feelings merely express an absence or surplus of water in the body, correctable through water fasts or strategies of soaking the body or hands in prepared water. A key premise of her theory is that water is the fundamental, and only reliable, recording agent of behavior. Water is thought to "see" and memorize the actions of persons. By filtering water through patients undergoing fits of various emotions, James creates supposed behavior water of these feelings that can be administered as medicine or antidote; a catalog of fluids that comprises a person's entire repertoire of behavior. James goes on to write about the centrality of water in considering the possibilities of the person in America (see *The New Water*), but warns of its danger, arguing that the next major war will be fought with water alone and that women should carry personalized water for protection, and consider water the only reliable diary, speaking their secrets privately into rivers, lakes, ponds.

1958

The Susan House, an experimental school for girls, has its beginnings in an all-girls' retreat conducted simultaneously one August evening in seven American towns. The focus of the retreats, initially, is to bury a clay head of Jesus, then meditate over the grave about the true requirements of the name of Susan, a technique of divination dating back to the Perkins Noise, when Perkins killed himself by vigorously repeating his own name, but not before achieving "immense information on the human enterprise." The Susan House school, initially conceived as a training ground for girls named Susan and no one else, gives rise to several specialty name-centered educational institutions and drives a new and terribly divisive political wedge into the population. Although many parents change the names of their children to Susan, only persons born into the name will be considered for enrollment (see *The Unwritten Books of Susan*).

1959

Animal artist George Rafkill, twenty-nine, is arrested when it is discovered that his popular portraits of horses and dogs, *The Animals of America,* which sell to hotels and restaurants, and can also be embroidered on flags, bear undeniable facial resemblances to thirteen women who have been missing from his Akron neighborhood for the past year. While Rafkill claims that he can "paint the dead," authorities point out that he only paints those dead that are also missing and believed murdered.

1963

Athlete Emily Anderson, forty-five, who has been imprisoned for interfering with runners at a men's track meet in Chicago just as they neared the finish line, is fatally injured when she is shot from a cannon into a brick wall during her "Hard to Die" show in July. An unknown Silentist, in a show of grief over the death of the quiet athlete, catapults herself from an English cliff into the sea, and an *Anderson* comes to be known as an act of mourning in which women launch themselves into the air for extended distances, often landing in the sea, but not necessarily.

1974

Men from Akron stack bones outside their houses to absorb the sound of women. When no bones are available, an entire person is used. Every family keeps a "Ben Marcus" for this purpose. Often he is sent out on thieving missions, smeared with a special scent, in order to attract the women's attention. Now the women are required by the Silence Commission to carry a small bone in a holster. If they wish to be heard, they must hurl the bone into a field, creating a current of deafness in the air. When men cough or talk into their hands, they are praying to their own bones. The women ride velvet-covered bone cages, called "horses." They produce an aggressive, highly pitched physical weeping, known as "galloping," and in this way spread their feelings across large fields of grass.

1978

The first plaster casting is taken of the inside of Bob Riddle's mouth, including the cavity that extends down his windpipe, ending at his lungs. When the casting is removed and hardens, it resembles a roughly shaped sphere (the inside of the mouth) with a ridged handle attached, and is considered a primary shape around which his body has grown, a hardened form of the white space at Riddle's center, a sculpture of his nothingness. Riddle calls it, incorrectly and rather pretentiously, his "soul," given that it represents his "language cave," and he argues that this shape is the primary object by which a person can be understood, and possibly controlled. The object will later be known as a Thompson Stick, as important a shape as the sphere or triangle. Silentists will quietly beat the earth with it, releasing pockets of sound that have been stored in the soil.

1979

Jane Marcus occurs in Deep Ohio. She has an accurate walking style and can converse in one language. She sleeps lying down, and uses a filter called "hair" to attract her mates. The small people in her house call her "Mother," and she answers them by collapsing the tension in her face, a release that passes for listening. Her motion is voice-activated. She has one pair of eyes, and they are often tired and red. When she uses her arms to prop up a document of regret, known as a "book," her bones form an ancient shape, and a brief flashing signal is sent out through the window and into the fields beyond her house, where the hive is.

Names

[Deborah]

THERE ARE ABOUT FIFTY known examples of it in the Rocky Mountain area, some dating as far back as 1931. They are thought to improve the people they encounter. The usual number of finished girls in a territory as common as "Deborah" is twenty-eight, with a quota of twenty and a maximum limit of thirty-two. Any more than this should suggest a dilution of the original Deborah, which produces strains of Amy or Ellen. Although the midcentury Rocky Mountain persons had utilized a Deborah to comfort the saddest local families, reserving the medical Deborah for only the most pressing cases of grief, the need for a cheer-spreading personage began to be felt at a national level, and abductions and faking occurred. There is consequently an extreme Deborah in the East, possibly of Colorado origin but bred through men of the Midwest (and therefore tall and reddish and chalky), dispensing a form of nearly unbearable, radical happiness into cities and homes. It is often housed in a little body, but its range is wide and its effect is lasting. To say "Deborah" is to admit to sadness and ask for help.

Statistics for Deborah: She preferred modifications to her head when we called her this. No matter how far we launched her in the chair, my sister did not faint. Small emotional showings were on view: contentment and pleasure, occasional cheer. She attempted to embrace my mother, usually before bedtime, and my mother only barely escaped these approaches. Sometimes she endured long hugs from this Deborah.

[Susan]

From afar, the Susan appears to be buckling, shivering, seizing, its body exhibiting properties of a mirage. Up close, there is mass to Susan and it is real to the touch. There will be food for you if you are Susan, although possibly a pile of food for Susan is a trap, to be regarded with suspicion. It is an elegant and refined system that established a school for itself, The Susan House. Its doctrine, The Word of Susan, is useful also to versions of Julia and Joyce but can be harmful to Judith. All of its books have gone unwritten.

Statistics for Susan: Quite poor weather during this phase. My sister aged considerably and showed signs of acute attention and superiority. Insisted on privacy. Dressed formally. Seemed not of our family. Our presence confused her. She once asked my father how he knew her name. It was a question my father could not answer.

[Jesus]

Women achieve their Jesus by speaking and studying their own name. The original Jesus figure examined his name, then derived actions and strategies from his analysis. This is the primary purpose of the Jesus noise—self-knowledge, instruction, advice. Women betray their Jesus when they forget that there is an answer at the heart of their name, to be divined by loud, forceful recitations of it in the streets, for as long as it takes. Simply saying "Jesus," however, is ineffective. (Breathing is the most common strategy for remembering our names.)

> *Statistics for Jesus:* It was decided not to call my sister this. Mother felt we might lose her. But I tried it anyway one night when my parents were asleep. I had to use a low-volume setting on the naming bullhorn and I whispered it at her while she slept. It was during an early Tina phase. She never woke. I sat at her bed all night and used this name against her until my mouth was exhausted. Nothing happened.

[Father]

To refer to a woman as "Father" is to engage her inner name and fill her hands with power. It is a code that many American women respond to with energy and hope. It is therefore used as a healing noise, particularly at hospitals, where nurses utter the word "Father" to women who are ill or tired. When men make love to Father, they use hearty motion and often call out words of labor and ecstasy; they thank Father, and they ask Father for more. Men in Utah, where this sort of naming is most frequent, take Father to the baths and hold her while rinsing her hair, until she feels soothed and calm, until she is manageable and not crazy with power, or too big for her body, or at least not dirty and alone, which makes Father dangerous. In wealthy households, Father enters a boy's room and blackens it with a gesture of her hand, then starts in on the boy with warm oil on his thighs, squeezing the oil into his legs until he weeps or breathes easy. Father pulls back the sheets and she climbs in to treat the boy and teach him to live. A boy often first makes love to Father because she is gentle and confident, someone the boy can trust. He holds on to Father's hands when she straddles the bed and affects her graceful motion. A boy says "Father" as she leans over him to help, dipping and rising, although sometimes the boy is quiet, preferring to feel her deepening attentions and not destroy the moment with speech.

> *Statistics for Father:* Chaos at the house. My real father was banished during this phase. He slept in the shed. I wanted to call him a girl's name, but I was not allowed to see him. My sister clearly thrived as Father: she boomed; she boasted; she tore through the house. She smashed the behavior television; she burned her old sleep sock. Mother was scared. A soothing litany of vowel songs was used on my sister to calm her down, without which she might have escaped. By the time the name would have worn off, she would have reached Akron. We restricted the study to two days. When we stopped calling her Father, she shed the hardest skin of all the names. My mother removed it from the house with a shovel before inviting my father back inside.

[Mary]

Every five minutes, a woman named Mary will stop breathing. It is a favorite of children, and every five minutes there are children standing in witness to the ending of Mary. Children clap at it when they see it. They are thrilled and they weep. Sometimes they become excited by a Mary that comes to die

before them and they chase it and hit it. The Mary takes a
wound. It holds up an arm and shields what is coming. It holds
a wound in its hand, and the children are delighted.

> *Statistics for Mary:* She was mostly slumped over. This was near
> the end. We tried to groom her, but her body was cold. Her
> hair broke when you touched it. She weakened visibly every
> time we said "Mary." She refused all food. In the mornings, she
> wrung her hands and wept quietly. Mother collected some-
> thing from her face. Possibly some scrapings, possibly the
> smallest bit of fluid. Mary was the last thing we called her. It
> was possibly the name that killed her.

[. . .]

Certain factions of women go by a nonname and therefore participate in a larger person that is little seen or heard or known.
It cannot be summoned or commanded. Generally, it walks
stiffly, owing to its numerous inhabitants. A body such as one
not named can be toppled, no doubt—felled and pinned to the
turf, brought under control with water and a knife, some rope,
and hard words. It is the primary woman, from which many
women have emerged, to which many will return. It is believed
to reside in Cleveland. Probably it is bleeding and tired. By
now, it might be nearly finished.

> *Statistics:* We treated my sister with silence at the end. We used
> an openmouthed name that failed to break the air, no different
> from a deaf wind. A great deal of hissing was heard in the
> house, though we could not find the source of this sound. My
> sister's skin was clear. It would not peel. It would not shed.
> We waited near her slumped body. She stayed nameless. She
> retained her skin.

5

The Launch

AT THE TIME OF THIS WRITING, I am going to be Ben's mother my whole life, no matter how extreme, inspired, or innovative my behavior. It is not a role I requested. My projects with emotion removal and silence would have thrived similarly without him. I do not seek your agreement on this topic. There was no invitation or application to this motherhood, only your oily body seeking to seal our obligations to each other. You intercoursed all over me in order to finally obligate me to you. I can't forget you with your back arched like a swan's, your teeth bared, clutching the sheets on each side of me as you funneled noiselessly between my legs, forgetting to breathe, until I felt you slowly wilting inside me, then a pool of dampness leaking down my bottom, which you asked me to stanch with your handkerchiefs. Your apologies afterward hardly made a difference. As soon as Ben was conceived, he was apologized for. A detail conveniently omitted from the prelaunch forecast we made when we cataloged our vision for the person he might become.

As much as I had hoped to court ambiguity, complication, and mystery regarding my basic relationship to Ben, to somehow annex my motherhood to my other projects, so that I was not merely shepherding another average person into the midwestern atmosphere, there is a fate that I am not imaginative enough to outdistance, a biology I have yet to surpass. I would like to alter it with chemicals. I would like to zero my heart, enter a silent house, and perform the gestures that will deliver me from all of the sameness. To be new in this awful, old job. I would like to outsmart the role that is destined for me. But I can't. I have failed to destroy my category.

Did I ask to be Ben's mother? I did not. Did I know that you were having sex with me? I did. Did I enjoy it? I did not. Encourage it? No. Did I realize that your rampant thrusting over my deliberately inert body would lead to a child such as Ben? I don't think so. Whose fault is it? Mine, of course. Is anyone else to blame? You are. Do I want something from you now? You'd better fucking believe it.

First, listen to what is happening to him; attend to my *decay narrative*. Next, note my requests of you. Note them. Note them. Note them. Last, learn what has been decided for you. One, two, three. Is there a punishment in store for you? Possibly, probably, awfully certainly. Yes. Better to think of it as a fate, a result, a consequence to what you did and didn't do. I mean to extract some final favors from you. You will soon see why you will be compelled to grant them. Pay attention.

Note: All quotes of you are taken from real things you said. I will quote you liberally. I will paraphrase you. I will channel your voice, imitate you. Since you apparently believe first and foremost in yourself, since you only subscribe to ideas of your own issue, I will allow your own words a front-and-center role. By pretending to be you, I will finally have you believe me. In case you get bored. In case you fool yourself into thinking another person's words, even your former wife's, are beyond, beneath, or beside your notice. Just in case. Put this aside at your peril. Read this at your peril. Do nothing at your peril. Breathe at your peril. No matter what, your peril will be the featured attraction of that portion of time we have been conservatively, cautiously, fearfully referring to as the future. If it is bad, and it hasn't happened yet, rest assured it will. You can look forward to it. At your absolute, total peril.

Now. Because we have withdrawn to opposite wings of the house this season, where we cannot audit the growth of our "son," or even gather at the behavior farm to chalk-talk an emotion-concealment style for his upcoming Akron debut, I am submitting a memorandum to you that demands your immediate attention. My concern is manifold and complicated and probably beyond your narrow comprehension. You need only know that my worry is for the boy we made together, who roves the Marcus property so cautiously, so breakably, that even our domestic animals could probably molest him for their own amusement.

Yes, you have visitation of Ben as part of the *Allotment for Father.* You ostensibly observe him at work and at play, alone, with others, asleep, at table, weeping, laughing, bleeding: the basic behaviors. But can I rely on you to be appropriately alarmed when Ben is less than average, inferior, loathsome, predictable? I cannot.

My aim is to forestall the demise of this new person we once shared ambition for. Although our launch objectives may have forked (yours into God knows where), we are each, I imagine, still vested in Ben's success enough to revise our separate child-rearing styles, which might ensure his feeble life at least through this season's behavior trials.

It is not appropriate—indeed, it is alarming—for a boy of Ben's age to be developing the hairline of a much older gentleman, and the apologetic body style of a low-riding dog. He appears to be someone who might more appropriately carry a cane, or use a walker to get himself comfortably from the couch to the toilet, if he even moves at all.

When Ben broods over his blocks or puzzle pieces, when he manipulates the domestic action figures you carved of him and his sister, or when he rotates the birds in his model aviary to reflect a religious system where birds act as transport vehicles for wind and prayer, I cannot help feeling I am watching a man who has, for some reason, based himself on a dead person. (Is it childish to believe that the more easily killable things of this world, most notably the birds, as delicate as lightbulbs, and seemingly randomly tossed aloft, have any agency? Is it childish to attach power to supposed objects of beauty? I only mean to establish whether Ben's nostalgia for birds might be useful in our ultimate plan for him.)

The goal, lest your exile has promoted yet further dementia in your defeated person, is still for him to launch into the greater Ohio—and whatever failing world lies beyond—with an unprecedented persona. I am not ashamed to want to make a boy who will one day set the mold for what might be called—if we gain any say over the conduct styles of our time—the New Behavior. If your goal is otherwise, or if, upon scrutiny of your strategies as an apparent man of Akron, you find that your fatherhood impulses have gone girlish along with your body—your trembling hands, your failing back, your dizziness and frequent wobbling, your sulking response when a conversation veers from your topic, exceeding your imagination or intelligence, your whimpering in your sleep, a list that barely touches on your array of feeble traits, which tempts me to create *an entire other document* cataloging your failures, a critical edition of my husband, an anthology of disappointments, a kind of best of the worst of the man I used to walk with, back when affection toward another person seemed like an answer to my own mediocrity, when a husband was just another blame hole—Ben will soon be removed from your part-time care and you might stop your reading here, pack your smart little bag, as if being ready for your journey will matter, and sit still until the quiet sisters knock on your door to remove you for all time from the visible world.

Knock, knock.

To the point: Things are getting worse with Ben, and I will soon overwhelm you with examples of his steady slide from excellence, his conspiracy against originality. Aside from a small, vanishing father, a difficult nutrition system meant to suppress or surface specific emotions, and an arsenal of equipment even two grown men would have trouble hauling around (helmets, packs, sleds, mouth-guards, grief biscuits, etc.), there are behavioral errors registering from our boy that were not in our forecast, wildly unchecked emotional displays that embarrass our household (though I would suggest that there can be no other *kind* of emotional display, and even the word "display," which in one of the major foreign languages means to spread one's ass cheeks as wide as possible without tearing the skin, should suggest the value of having emotions at all). These are detours of his person that we failed to map in advance. What is unknown about Plan Ben, or previously unpredicted, is unacceptable. It bespeaks an imprecise launch, and, as such, invites our quickest mastery. "To parent," in Greek, means "to know." I think. In German, it means "to cut trees, clear a path, and invite people into the space you have made." The French use the word "father" for "failure." "Dad" means "an underwater passage to the afterlife, a constricted tube, a drowning pipe." Access is difficult. There will be water everywhere. You could drown midway. "Ben" means "never; not on your life; you're out of your mind." "Ben" means "the best I could do." In some cultures, the word serves as an apology.

Let's examine how well we've lived up to these terms.

On those difficult evenings when the parenting schedule requires me to touch our young man's head in a Mothering Action before putting him to sleep, under the labored shushing sounds of the Ideal Breathing tape broadcast into his bedroom, hissing, hissing, hissing, rendering his room like a wind tunnel, I sense his skull to be smaller than that of other boys, softer and shapeless and altogether too fragile for my liking.

Correct me if I'm wrong, but his head should not conform to his mother's hand, even a hand that could once repel an advancing, trouserless husband, a man who deployed actual military circlings on his approach to our shared bed, techniques from an actual book, requiring me to be similarly strategic in resisting his attempts at the aggression he called intimacy, the chafing lurches into my body that caused his face to collapse with relief. Yet to battle this man (you) was also to accidentally touch his bare legs and bottom and crotch as he conducted his wagon circle of my overtired person, leaving me to effectively only fight the top half of him, the clothed half, or else possibly incite his arousal even further, a handicap that resulted in a woman (myself) who learned how to beat a man's trunk, his arms, his face, while avoiding all that lay below.

Case in point: The neighboring Smith children, when they pile over the south fence, and commence to lower their heads and charge the wall that encircles the listening hole, seem only temporarily stunned by the collision. Apart from questioning their aim in such a pursuit (namely, why would a young Smith risk what is arguably its best asset—its head—in order to knock down a wall that it could easily surmount with a ladder; what could be the launch objective of the Smith parents in allowing such a battery to occur, particularly on someone else's property?), one must observe that there are no blackouts among that bunch of youngsters, no fainting, no discernible concussions, contusions, or spells. Just a white cloud stunned from the wall by the ramming of their heads, rendering the Smiths as dark shapes inside a haze, blaring like foghorns as they wait for clear air (a bluster that must challenge the decoding tactics of our young listeners laboring in the hole). The Smiths roughhouse as though they were smash puppets, and one observes no resulting decay in their persons, whereas our Ben, let us confess, flinches if his own hand comes too near his face, as with eating, for example (he is too facially cautious to feed himself soup; we have lately resorted to a blindfold), or grooming (I observed him fastening his hairbrush to the wall, his arms keeled back while he burrowed his head against it, as though truffling for some message in the bristles that might rub off on his face). He is so shy of himself that he often ducks his own motions while leaving the house or carrying seeds to the Storm Needle, as if a bee were dive-bombing his face and his hands had produced a sign language to ward it off. If he continues to smother his own actions, he will simply be a boy who spins in place, erasing every gesture he makes until he is busily still, a kind of hummingbird person at best, fascinating to watch, but in the end just another curiosity, merely pitiable. While such a repertoire might suffice if he were a dancer, parodying the way people sabotage their own progress, a palsy meant to ridicule the very idea of motion, as a person it is not acceptable for his actions to symbolize, even satirically, the failures of others. The parallels are too chancy, and our Akron neighbors should not be expected to supply all of their own irony, to comprehend that Ben represents something other than himself, which was never our intention for him. We seek to put people in mind of absolutely nothing when they observe him. We desire primary behavior from our boy. Let him be new, or let us remove him from the yard, the house, the world.

Okay, problem articulated. Now, Ben's mania toward his own head is evidence of something, but what? He is either afraid of himself (not exactly irrational, and in some sense impressively shrewd of the boy to identify his own self as a threat, a discovery that takes other people years, if they make it at all), or he's instinctually protecting his head from harm, which is one more boring way he is just like All Other People to This Date, not just weak and death-prone but glaringly, theatrically weak, almost asking to be killed. My feeling? Do not, do not, *do not* fuck around and ask for something like that. It is too damn tempting. At least *pretend* to want to live.

It is not that I presumed the girls' water we used as his infant formula would counteract these predictable, unsatisfactory instincts (protect the head, breathe, eat, grab warm bodies, and nuzzle their flesh). For all of its power, girls' water cannot prevent basic animal responses to threats or hunger, however boring these predicaments have proved to be. As you may have noted from your observation tower, I have stood outside under the flood of evening birds, who circle the emotion furnace and feed on the behavior smoke, and I have consumed great amounts of water, with the hope of generating an ideal learning fluid for the boy, which would save him from the terrible guesswork of life among people. He drinks it and he smiles, but nothing is learned; he swallows no instructions. Ben still sits at the window and sings his warble, runs after the birds with his little arms waving as though he controls them with string. I am trying to discourage his sense that he can influence the life around him, that he is responsible for something that is already occurring. Part of my approach here is the institution of a Powerlessness Emphasis Program. For about an hour each day that Ben is charged to me, I take him around the house and point out things he was not responsible for, mostly tables, chairs, beds, walls, other people. I have lately also been scheduling a stop at the mirror by the bathroom, allowing Ben to discover how unremarkable his features are, to educate him on the basic disappointments of the face. When the light is right, I drop his pants and we consider how crushed and matted his hips appear, how his penis looks like an entire person smushed into a wrinkle, his buttocks like the flattened head of a seal.

My problem: Parenthood should not feel like charity. Ben is proving special in the wrong way. My soft spot for cretins is bone-hard.

I am nevertheless disappointed to see Ben's contract with

poor performance so quickly fulfilled, his apparently easy assim-
ilation to other people and their average theater of disappointments, despite our best efforts to originalize him.

My concern: by publicizing his "insecurity" (your words),
Ben boasts of a future failure and creates a zone of foreshad-
owing around his head, indicating his Kill Spot, akin to wearing a bull's-eye. I read the papers enough to know that failure
is the trend for young people today, but it does not compel me,
and I'll be curious to watch its enticements fade as success and
survival regain prominence as the coveted actions for persons,
and others, of our time. A sort of glory is lately attached to
coming up short, then articulating the inadequacy, soliciting
blame with the same fervor our generation sought to deny
it, as though verbal eloquence can overwhelm incompetence.
But I say let the other American children fail and brag of
failure, whether through song or verse, even exaggerating
the various ways they have become terribly weak people of
the Current Moment, a regime where the word "person" now
equals "loss," where to breathe is to inhale remorse. Error is a
dead end. Modesty is the most arrogant stance of all. Our boy
will continue to operate in secret, beyond the behavior fads,
and his debut will revise what has heretofore been thought
possible in the scope of actions that a person can produce. I
believe this.

Do I care how arrogant this sounds? I do not. Am I worried
that my ambitions for him are not his ambitions for himself? I
am not. Left to his own devices, Ben would have no devices.
Left alone, he would be alone. The history of behavior has
borne this out. No more equivocating. My role is to optimize
him, to medicate his trajectory, to fuel the launch. "To mother:"

a verb suggesting special, strategic assistance, a tactic of person making. Mothering is the science of waking up. Bestowing behaviors on others. Mothering.

So how will he do it? At the least, Ben should be outfitted with a decoy weakness, an area some distance from his head, that he nurses with care. This is an old-fashioned idea, but one that we have apparently overlooked in all of our quests for newness. I am not suggesting a garden—civilization should quit its relentless tilling of the earth before it digs its way to hell; it is presumptuous the way people attempt to enhance or alter vegetal life, while in the end they only interfere with something they don't understand (fatherhood, according to my father, is to modulate interference, to ration intervention, like management with a whip). Instead, why not a living creature who can die before Ben does, to give Ben a sample of recoverable loss, just to widen his arc of grief before his emotions are finally cleansed? But who or what should this living creature be? Who or what? Who or what? Do any candidates come to mind that we can sacrifice to Ben's advancement? A loved one? A formerly loved one? A despised one who thinks he's a loved one? Think! Presuming your own selfishness still obtains (which isn't even a presumption, but a rational prediction based on all of your past behavior), and you refuse to completely and finally donate your own person for this project, we might consider accessorizing Ben with a dog or a child, a sidecar diversion to give his potential attackers real blood to shed and to let Ben fail at something grave—the upkeep of another life—without dying himself, though we should be careful not to fetishize his survival above more spectacular behavioral gains. Let's not presume that he needs to live to be considered a successful young man. Survival for its own sake can tend to feel so obvious, so plainly desperate.

A short diagnosis of Ben's condition: Afraid of One's Own Motion, Afraid of Hands, Scared to Breathe, Walking Fear, Repulsion Toward Food, Fear of Clouds, Water Phobia, Nauseated by Sound, Allergic to Objects, Allergic to People, Allergic to Oneself. I presume parents, if anyone, should cure these fears and aversions. Parents should intervene at a stage such as this one and impart a survival tactic, a motion reduction, an anxiety channel to siphon off the distracting behavior. Certain specific parents, in fact, should consider the ultimate sacrifice to their son, a boy who might finally require the loss of a parent in order to be healed (I'll spell it out: Ben requires a disappeared father, a dead father, a father harmed and brought to his knees, an embarrassed or humiliated father, a father attacked, a father lost at sea, a father with no money, a depraved father, a shot-in-the-head father, a gut-shot father at night, a father fallen from a tree, winded, a confused and possibly blind father, groping down the hallway in his nightshirt, entering the wrong room, weeping, a father who must be fed, a deaf father, whose lips curve around other people's words but never discern them, a father who one day doesn't wake up, who stiffens there in bed, finished). A successful young boy might require one of these events to mark him as a more authentic young man, a man with experience, a man with knowledge, a man who has suffered. If you cared at all for his progress in the world, you would help Ben with this deficiency; you would not even blink before volunteering. You would be loading your gun at this very moment. You would be swallowing all of the wrong pills and dragging your fatally poisoned body out into the field, where Ben could watch you fail this world forever, and never forget your death. A father having a seizure. A father expiring in the grasses outside his own home. How proud we would all be if you could do this for him! What an amazing gift! How noble, to exit your hard life and infuse our young man with such an important, defining loss! How many young men actually get to watch their fathers die? An intelligent man would overcome his self-serving blind spot on this topic. What exactly are you "living" for if not to accelerate your son's stalled launch, to jettison your sorry boy back onto the frontier of the all-new behavior? Let him live through grief! An intelligent man would do this.

For my part, no matter how often I provoke the boy to a fainting spell by launching his body in the chair—his limbs wheeling in the air above the fainting tank, my own son aloft and unconscious, confusing the bird life in the vicinity—upon landing, his fear of himself is not cleansed. During the resuscitation procedure, after I salt his upper lip, he comes to alertness and seems "glad" to be alive, for I observe his face to gain the rictus of a smile and I watch his arms breach the space toward my person as he nuzzles into my heat, his mouth transmitting coos and baby sounds. But after I right his body, and distance myself two arm's lengths from him to better observe the effects of the faint, and then note his symptoms in the ledger, he is soon again fending some invisible attack near his eyes, swatting the air, sometimes appearing to hug himself lightly on the shoulders in a solo embrace, as though his arms were being operated from afar and he were administering to himself some early, unchecked version of affection. I am repulsed when comfort becomes the chosen performance of the day, when people decide to soothe one another or themselves. It is so disappointing to ratify our panic. And to try to comfort oneself, a sort of asexual masturbation, like administering a massage to your own body, simply communicates to others what they should never do for you. It advertises your basest need. If Ben desires to be touched by me, he certainly won't get his wish by touching himself in my presence. That is simply patronizing and far too obvious.

As you know, I prefer objects that do not give when you push or poke or prod them: a wall, a rock, a tower. I prefer men who don't fall down and weep, who absorb a blow, who do not scamper and yell when chased, but stand firm, crouch, square off, meet an attack with something like resistance, even if it kills them. The four-point stance is my favorite posture for men. It indicates readiness, disguises fear, and raises their bottoms above their heads, which more authentically prioritizes a man's body. Men should not gust so heavily from the mouth when they are being tended to; their noises should occur as language, or not at all. I do not like their sounds of relief. They sigh too easily, overusing the facial strategy of "smiling," as though communicating their mood will deliver wanted news from their persons. As though, as though. They expect a far more ample interest in their needs than is ever warranted. The biggest tactical error of our time: using the face to communicate a mood. It amounts to spying on oneself. As for men, it is their completely wrong view of themselves I cannot stand. We could use a little more self-loathing from them, to give the rest of us a break. There is so little accuracy in their faces.

So when I can preside over the alteration of an object, or when that object sympathizes with my touch so much as to yield to it (Ben's personality, so-called, not to mention his body, such as it is, and his head, his overall yieldingness and suscepti-bility and failed resistance to everything suggested for him), I am inclined, since I pursue my desires with "intense behav-ior" (your words), to continue shaping that object until it is small enough for me to stash in my pocket or bury or fling into the sea, all actions that would bring a final harm to Ben and our plan.

Although I am eager to resist the stereotypes of motherhood that would have me coddling the boy, swathing him in blan-kets, soothing his rages with my special, medical voice, and con-firming or accommodating every fear and worry he attempts to indulge, I am not convinced that the opposite Approach of Indifference is any more original a parenting stance, and I'd like to resist ignoring the young man just because it's a less charted region of behavior, however personally fascinating I might find it, however endlessly rich the results it might yield for me. Detachment is an indulgence of mine, I'll admit, par-ticularly when Ben speaks to me—announcing his feelings, querying mine, reporting what he has observed in the field, strategies that all cause me to stiffen—and I must moderate the display of my aloof postures with vigilance, lest it seem to him that I am simply powered down, or drunk. As useful as it is to position myself as a remote, masterful mother who employs hidden, satellite controls while refusing her son such techniques as physical proximity, or basic verbal or physical acknowledgments of his messages or gestures, such as eye contact (an overrated method), the danger is that, however advanced his mind might become as a result, Ben's body will cool considerably, he will grow inert, his muscles will atrophy, and he will become too listless even for the most basic self-care. A dead son is not immediately in our interest at this time.

The question now is, So What? Here is just another crisis of parents with an average kid who will not produce the behaviors they dream about. Welcome to the club. What is so different about our struggle? Why should we complain when our boy fails to pioneer? Should we not be pleased by his divergence, even a divergence into likelihood, sameness, average output? Is it not necessary for him to be *precisely other* than we thought he would, exactly outside of our imagination for what people can do, a schism that defines the tension produced between generations? Well, yes. In theory, I agree. Let Ben be a Dutch princess. How utterly startling. My problem, which I hope is yours as well, is that Ben's failure has not proved challenging, surprising, mysterious, complicated, difficult, alarming, or exciting. He is small and colorless and his voice cannot compete with a hushed room. His words, when he uses them, are nervous. He is bald and his head is overlarge. His lips are fat and wet.

Which is where you come in.

I am not sure if, in your ministrations to him, when you cleanse him or coach his life maneuvers on the Person Course behind the shed, you have had cause to handle his face, or to read his gestures with your mitten to discover what our young man might be feeling (not that such a subject concerns you, or should). But I ask that you look to him at once during his next behavior bath, being careful, please, not to alarm him, if indeed he is not accustomed to hosting your hand on that part of his body (reminder: Ben has Afraid of Hands).

Here are some remedy queries you might consider during your examination:

Should a boy's face be that soft?

Does overnight burial harden a boy's head?

Will an Outdoor Endurance Occasion create a facial callus sufficient to conceal him into adulthood?

Does such a callus permanently guarantee an emotionless citizen?

Can a controlled flame be used to toughen his face and generate a gesture-free armor for him?

Next, where exactly is that "music" coming from, if not his mouth? I'm sure you've heard it, unless you are as deaf to relevant sounds (your wife's voice, your son's voice, your own ludicrous voice) as you sometimes seem, a low keening pitch off his body that attends his person in the daytime, like a morose sound track? ("Morose" is probably not the right word. Just to say that a boy's body is projecting its own sound track should be enough of a description, and types of music are reportedly subjective |a topic outside my expertise|, so when I say it's morose, I'm only revealing the ways in which I allow myself to be sad; it becomes a tool for others to overthrow me. Meaning: Enemies of mine |fill in the goddamned blank| could use Ben to make me sad, when even his rough breathing sounds like an old German dirge. They could station him near my bed while I sleep, and dose me with a hard sadness. They could position pictures of him on my shelves and within my personal effects, leading me to pause throughout my day and spiral into nonuseful contemplation of his face, which still invites interpretation, no matter how finally I have learned to ignore the gestures living there, to never look at Ben's face, for fear of the trap there. Let me say more specifically that properties of this music arising off our son's body are able to surmount my current Grief Defense Strategy, which I admittedly developed far too late in life to be effective around the clock. My shield is down sometimes just before a meal. Moments of hunger seem somehow tied to moments of feeling. The precise relationship between the two eludes me.)

Nevertheless, nevertheless, nevertheless. Some questions for you: Should Ben's tones be transcribed by our listener (using twelve-tone behavioral notation) and then sent to a musicologist for interpretation?

Is it safe to make an audiotape of the young man, and if so, where against Ben's body, or elsewhere, should the microphone be placed?

What are the bootleg risks for such an endeavor?

Could a clever parent or person-producing company (don't fucking get me started) divine information about a person like Ben based on the sound of his body, and do we then run the risk of a person-dilution duplication, a behavior theft, in case his person is sampled and stored and broadcast for the benefit of other families, who were too lazy to raise a boy of their own, who were too stupid, who couldn't be bothered to think for even one second about what it was they were doing in creating a brand-new person, that no one in the world had ever laid eyes on, so why not steal the very details and parameters and attributes of the person they're calling Ben Marcus?

Do we leak details about our boy by allowing others to hear the sound of his body before we officially release him to view?

By publishing such sounds from our Storm Needle on a clear day, when person sounds will travel unobstructed as far as the state border, as clear as birdcalls, do we compromise our New-ness Incentive and contribute to the derivative child-rearing styles of America?

And, ultimately, will learning something new about Ben end up mattering? Is it healthier to maintain, even to cultivate, a degree of mystery about the boy, so that we ourselves will not lose interest in him? Can we find out too much? Or should we strive to lose interest, in the economic sense, so as to zero our own panic in case he does emerge as a bold and altogether hard-core person with an approach to the world that might ulti-mately harm our own physical selves?

I have stopped short of fully disrobing the boy to finally trace the source of the sound, and the Quiet Sisters seem shy of him when his person is so loud (producing person evasions, fainting onto body rugs when he passes, hiding under cloth when he speaks, weeping if he eats grain). A young girl here, operating covertly under the name Julie, performed an Ander-son out of the widow when Ben's volume grew too unbearable.

I assure you that I am not afraid, in the technical sense, of hosting a version of Ben that is naked, particularly if it means discovering tactics that might be crucial to his future. Some-times, while scrubbing my face before undergoing the Posture Hour with Jane Dark, I might entertain a memory of the very young and undersized Ben, who, as I'm sure you'll recall, was often unattired in our midst. Dark's Posture Hour is a strenu-ous regimen that always seems to disarm my thought stream and render me susceptible to nonuseful recollections, and the mandatory facial scrubbing beforehand only accentuates this vulnerability. (Is the face more important than we had thought? Should it be scrubbed more vigorously, scoured, brushed? By assaulting our own faces, do we possibly somehow access all-new behaviors? Should we tear off our faces? Should we cut them free with a knife? Is there something under there?) But I recall that Ben was a baby nudist, who showed no instinct for clothing and seemed inclined, like a young buccaneer, to stride across the living room in such a manner as to foreground his sharp, angular genitals, his penis slashing here and there, often cutting the fabric barriers we'd slung from the rafters to deter his free passage within a cloth-made world: hips forward, probing the wind, arms folded behind his back, his bottom tucked so far under him that it appeared as a gaping seam up his puckered front side. His behavior was a sort of vaudeville youth pornography that came from nowhere, as though he were puppet master of his own penis, conducting it through flight patterns that seemed nearly impossible. Where did someone so young learn to make such a horror of his own crotch? He had seen no movies and read no books; in fact, he was only recently free of his life-prevention hood, the cotton bunting meant to limit his experience of the world. Was such a display consciously designed to alarm his young mother?

So you'll understand if I feel that his nudity is too emotion-ally treacherous for the women here who might encounter it. The nudity of a young man can lead to a wide range of emo-tions, most notably disappointment. And, however much I subscribe to long seasons of vague disappointment, accompa-nied by a low-chain starch diet to suppress my desires, disap-pointment produces a listless clientele, a sluggish workforce. Even as a sire, Ben was not required to fully disrobe (why complicate sexual collaboration with full nudity, introducing curiosity and repulsion all at once, a combination that all but shuts down the reproductive organs?). Not to mention that Ben could only sustain an erection if it poked through the unzipped fly of his denims, a fact I am reminded of every time I encounter a pair of his buttoned, unzipped trousers in the hamper, encrusted about the fly area with excess albumen. Even with his pants at his ankles, his concentration flagged and he lost his temper, and while the denim ringlet you designed acted briefly as a tumescence sustainer, or, in the Spanish parlance, a "cock ring," it seemed far less cumbersome to let him operate his fornications through his zipper hole, though his blue jeans were chafing to so many of our young women here. Just one more reason there was so little conception in the house that winter.

Being his father, at least for these last days, I hope you might assume the task of disrobing Ben to sleuth a possible torso sound hole, and report to me what you discover. If you anticipate experiencing bouts of sudden loss while encountering a nude young man—your body seized by "plummet mode" though indeed you remain seated, a sure sense of descent gripping your skin, a vertical wind shaving up your legs, you will do best to conceal these sensations from our boy. Attire yourself properly in the sterilized examiner's equipment, a doctor's smock, and shoe guards. Visor yourself, or wear your hood. But in the end, it is not for me to tell you what to do with *unbidden emotions* (is that a redundant phrase?), or outsized reactions to the basic consorting styles between men, as with, in this case, a large man disrobing a small boy to discover the source of a mysterious sound, leading to your loss of breath, your frozen hands, your back seized up, your total body collapse, your Deep Regret, which actually feels like a blood condition and not just an emotion. It is so petty to feel things just because you can, and to indulge in feelings you might like to call "strong," and to then be proud of what you call your "ability to feel," as though it were a talent. As though, as though. He is your boy and his body is modeled after yours, apprenticing it while introducing improvements so subtle we could never guess at them, however much we believe ourselves to be *raising* him. To raise: to flay off skin and insert another body inside the pelt. From the perspective of relevancy, your response to Ben is no longer interesting. You would do well to remember that your reaction to our son is anecdotal at best. You showed long ago that feelings couldn't be proved. Should you now live by your own lesson? You should. Should you live at all? We'll see.

The real alarm: Even with the clear helmet you've introduced to Ben's wardrobe (let's see that more youth pay attention to his equipment, if not his tendency to weep during field events), he seems highly breakable and far too temporary a person, and I should like at once to rectify our home atmosphere so that our young man might at least breathe enough air to promote his little body toward a more common manhood, armored against those small dull birds that clog our Ohio airways and seem a little bit too interested in Ben's passage, trailing his sloping body like a long black kite whenever he leaves the house to stick his unmistakable and prematurely bald head into public airspace for anyone to see it. (Isn't there a famous old story about a boy who is followed by birds from city to town to country, until he is running into the woods, the birds not far behind? In the story, doesn't the boy finally hide underground, where the relentless birds can't go, though they try anyway by crashing into the earth at the perforation of the boy's disappearance, leaving an ever-growing smear of beak and feathers in the soil? Does the boy not meet a terrible end underground, a place so dark that his body has been twisted upside down for weeks, before his head, so fruity with blood, grows too enriched, too large? Is the phrase "terrible end" also a redundancy? And if there is such a famous old story, what exactly are we to deduce from Ben's apparent casting in it? Was the character's name also Ben? Did he die? Why would our Ben be taking part in a story that was written down long ago? Do the stories repeat themselves, or is Ben being derivative?)

Request: Can your team, or what's left of it (these are such quiet days in Men Town), not devise a limbering station for Ben to visit each day before breakfast, on such days when you are his Learning Host? For my part, I would be willing to surrender my commitment to Dark's Ninety Motions™ as the ideal actions for a body. I realize that Ben is a boy, though I take issue with your definition of this word, and I defer now to any movement at all you might choose for your last sessions with him, so long as that movement does not confiscate him in a Final Exit.

You're wondering now whether this note to you is itself only an articulate set of complaints, a description of a crisis, lacking in target behaviors, solutions, or rectification approaches. You're also wondering—let me keep guessing—why I would write to you at all, given my "complete control of Ben" (your words), my "mastery over the launch" (your words), my profound disregard for your strategies and designs for the person-building program initiated with respect to Ben, though the phrase "strategies and designs" rather overstates the coherency of your thinking on this project. Why include you or ask for your help, and in the same breath ridicule you and threaten your life? One answer: Such a contradiction is mysterious. I don't seem like I should need your help, yet I am asking for it. Possibly I mean to put you off guard, or to give you hope. Or I am just as selfish as you'd like to believe, and I need your exclusive wisdom regarding Ben, no matter how much I might publicly disavow your role with him. I seek your counsel in private, then ridicule you in public. This interpretation flatters your pride, and I certainly don't mind if you entertain it, however deeply wrong it actually is. (It is in my interest for you to be wrong about me. The less you understand, the more attention you will pay.)

One theory:

Mastering a launch, as every parent tries to do, also requires ceding control, hard as this is, portioning tasks to deputy figures, however weak these assistants might be, designating partial or temporary authority to Field Decoys (you) who might influence the trajectory of the subject (Ben) in small but significant ways, who are poised in small but significant ways to supplement the far more complicated work of the launch master herself, a person, in this case, who must cover such a wide range of problems and challenges that her actual hands-on work with the subject must often be farmed out to helpers with a smaller horizon of concerns, who can then report back to her and describe the tactile sensations of handling her child, interacting with him, witnessing the behavior he produces throughout the day, which is information she still requires to perfect her work, though, because she has already touched her child, and has no time or patience for repetition, she only requires reminders and updates that can easily be delivered by her staff. Much of her contact with her actual boy can be verbal, secondary. A launch master is concerned to be not just a mother but also a behavior creator, a consultant, and ultimately a specialist in the horizon, an expert in the distance, which is the final problem of the young person in America. She sculpts his ending while he has barely begun. She scouts so far ahead that sometimes her child cannot even see her. Forget about tethers and leashes and kiddy cords; a launch master takes full advantage of the so-called generation gap. She swings wide. The furthest distance between two points is a mother. Although she may appear as a speck in the distance, she is in reality huge and looming. She is the expanse, not the point. This distinction will be meaningless to you, which only illustrates how out of your league you are.

We have carpentry uses for you. We have construction uses for you. There are projects in the physical plant that could use your help. Read on if you are concerned to participate in the world we are building for Ben.

What I suggest first is the introduction of windows into Ben's room in Man House, a ventilation system that will not leave him so flushed and lightheaded; and possibly, at least for one learning season, a modest tank-and-mask affair that he might harness over his helmet just to get him back on his feet without choking and fainting as often.

If you agree to aid us, you have my permission to travel to the women's side of the compound for a parts consultation at the shed, though I don't mean to imply that you lack the facilities to produce a streamlined child's mask yourself. Only know that I think our staff, if you have any people left who still answer to you, can collaborate on this dilemma without too much rupture, particularly if the treaty is observed.

If you do make your way over here, I ask that you observe the motion laws, travel during daylight, and resist carrying weapons or bringing your so-called assistants. If Larry emerges, you can trust that he will be fired upon until he ceases his advance. Then his body will be seized. All captures will be filmed, and the films will be projected on the barn as a caution. Let's not have any more trouble. I'm sure you've seen the trucks behind the house, gouging into North Yard, and the Quiet Sisters at work digging the hole, and I'm further sure I don't need to tell you that this hole, *like certain holes, called "graves," built to house the dead,* can and will serve many interesting purposes, including the possible containment of figures failing to yield to former agreements.

That was certainly a mouthful of a sentence. You might favor yourself by reading it again for clues.

Or in plain speech: Watch yourself.

Let me now describe a change in my beliefs, not interesting in its own right, but certainly bound to affect the so-called future moments of Ben, the only real topic to bind us at this late moment in your conscious life.

While I once agreed that limiting Ben's use of natural elements—rationing his light, air, and water, concealing his food, ironizing or curtailing the affection we dispensed (employing such techniques as the hug that just misses, the air kiss, the parent mannequins, the empty house in the morning, the growling sound track piped into his room at night, the wolf experience, the cruel girl in the field)—would theoretically create a hungrier, sharper, strong lad—better suited to become the kind of person we once agreed we would like to launch, a boy who only relied on natural resources as a last resort, in case a sound-out or blackout or food minus really did seize the current moment, or in case the current moment itself contracted and went airless and commenced to suffocate those persons living in it (as you predicted every day over breakfast, when words of doom were apparently once thought to render a young family dependent on the man who spoke them)—my team and I are discovering that the once-intriguing deprivations might now be too severe for Plan Ben, tiring the actual Ben's little body beyond use, caving in his chest, withering his legs. In short, we are actually only teaching him exhaustion, fatigue, despair, and he is a very quick study, for he is becoming almost like some figure from literature: short of breath, despondent, frail, contrived.

A "body bellows," as you call it, is undoubtedly an important way to teach a man to earn his own life, something I still favor, theoretically. But I have a question: When do these devices exceed Ben's Opponent Quota, and how many enemies to his natural sustenance can he rightfully engage before he loses the battle to become an upright man during the daytime? Are parents not enemies enough? In other words: Is our family project still interesting if Ben dies beneath a burden of homemade equipment? Does a child-rearing strategy effectively terminate when the child does? Is it possible that you are scheming to induce an exit in your child because you sense one impending for yourself, thus you have straitjacketed him with a bellows set on "high" and he is gently commencing to expire? And, if so, would that not be a somewhat derivative approach to the art of the launch? Is it not ultimately dull to abort your own launch? Are you so boring that you would try to kill Ben? Have you eschewed excellence simply because your own project as a man has failed?

Make no mistake; I do remember your early work, if this

consoles you at all, though my intention is to be correct, rather than to comfort you. It was fatherly of you to suit up in the body bellows yourself before apprenticing Ben to the project, though, if you'll recall, young Ben steered himself well clear of his thus-attired father, and even I suffered more than my typical indifference touching you that month (yet the bellows did provide a difficulty that I had previously found your body to lack: Navigating the apparatus made me impatient enough to almost desire you, when your body was rendered inaccessible due to the wires that bound it). In those days, you could barely breathe, and often lay gasping on the floor, your eyes tearing, your skin a flat and terrible shade of blue. That was when our eroticism followed a medical model, me nursing you as though you were a huge and faulty mechanical bird, come crashed near my home, brave and stupid and near death, allowing the hardest kind of love, which would not have to be backed up in the morning. I could mythologize you beyond a walking mediocrity, a flesh-made disappointment. You were my broken machine, a cage with blood flowing through it.

It is true that when you finally shed the bellows that early spring day down at the learning pond, there was something buoyant, if spastic, to your step, an odd and mismanaged freedom your body struck with the air, as though you would be more at home ballooning over Ohio alongside the clouds, a man to lead the weather out of our lives for good, some sort of pied piper pulling wind behind him. You had clearly become stronger, but it was not clear to what end, and this sums you up entirely: intriguing and original upon first glance, yet useless and vain in the end, a reminder of another pointless way life could have gone, and actually did go, but not before, thankfully, thankfully, I altered my own course wide, wide, wide from you, and got myself the hell out of your wrongful way.

It puts me in mind of an instructive moment when I was a girl. There was a boy who was a runner, whose mother wanted terribly for him to win the races. Every morning we saw him jogging in his medical shorts through our neighborhood, a tall boy with a father's portion of hair on his arms. While we girls were hidden in greatcoats, our scarves wired around us and hats stoppered on our heads, foolish lunches handed over that we would later trade for candy, this boy was steaming with fog as he ran down our streets, just about on pace with the cautious little cars that boxed us up to school. But all of the boy's training didn't put him ahead, because there was inevitably some other boy in another town who could run faster, and did, repeatedly, in race after race. Our boy was not a winner, and his huge desire to win only seemed to embarrass everybody, because his confidence in himself was so inaccurate.

Then, revelation, his mother decided to handicap his training so that during races he would have more power. The first handicap was an oxygen tank that limited his breath. Come race time, having shucked his gear, he was not only pounds lighter but it was as if he had a sudden third lung, a power boost akin to cutting gills into his ribs. After that, he ran like an escaped lung patient, the tank on his back bobbing like an oversized coffee thermos.

He was faster, but still not enough.

Next, she hooked a cart to her boy, had him run like a mule carrying fruit to market. Except instead of fruit there was a man in the back of that cart who did things to impede the boy's progress.

Things?

He heckled him. He pulled on his "reins." Objects were tossed in his path. There was some occasional tackling.

The cart, too, failed to improve his performance, though it certainly complicated it and introduced new ways for him to thrive. Had there been a cart-pulling race, our boy would have taken first place. He could run under duress. If there was ever a war, for instance. Et cetera.

Next, she abandoned constraining her son's body and took him off the roads entirely. She went in for visualization, had him picturing stuff that hadn't happened, to prepare his body for when it would. He was entirely on blocks, stretching out his brain. Our boy stopped running down our streets and we no longer saw him, except when he was a normal citizen in the classroom, plain and powerless. I remember how disappointed I felt watching him do math. I refused to accept him as a citizen, so dull in his school uniform. Someone said that each day before and after school he sat in a "running room" his mother had designed, thinking about running. I pictured his brain fat with thought, his scalp pale, his drumstick calves pulsing with unbidden twitches.

The result at his next race was surprising. He was serene, calm, sort of floating along, driven not by his legs, it seemed, but by some strange current of energy the air had sent into him alone on the racing course. A mind-powered runner. It was beautiful to watch him. If you squinted, you could almost see thin strings of light feeding his muscles as he ran. He had grown slightly thick at the waist, and his legs had lost their veiny, snakelike strength, yet the other runners looked crippled next to him, awkward and near death, as though he were the only man on a gassed battlefield who could breathe. He brought a lyricism to the art of motion that made everyone at the race nervous to even try to walk. I felt stupid and ashamed and my hips ached. It hurt just to stand there. I creaked and cracked on my sockets as though my bones were made of cookie. The result of the race? His original style proved unwinning. He came in third. Speed seemed irrelevant to his gestural fluidity. He was getting worse.

His mother was perplexed. She had fetishized his rehearsal, mistakenly believing that people practice, physically or mentally, for some event in the future. Her solution stunned everyone in the neighborhood, however, and I credit her remedy with solving my own already-erring emotions at the time.

Here's what happened: His mother decided to train for him. She had not been helping him directly enough, had made no sacrifice of her own whatsoever. There had always been the two of them, but only *he* had been training. So this time the boy stayed home and his mother did the running. She was weak and fat and out of shape. She lacked the flashy gear. Mostly, she trained in a long denim baking skirt, her hips jostling like sacks of flour tied around her waist. We could very nearly walk faster than she ran, but we stayed away and watched her circling their block, sometimes all day on weekends, while the boy watched through binoculars from the window, tied down with weights, noting God knows what in a ledger. Sometimes at night, we could still hear her sharp, chipping steps and her breath, as painful and awkward as someone might produce if her head was wrapped in plastic.

Clearly, she wasn't showing her boy how to run. So what was she doing? How could her pained, palsied trotting possibly help him get faster? Her running itself would never help him; it was what her running led to—namely, her death one morning several weeks into her training, right in front of the house, the boy positioned at his perch in the window (some would say he was chained there). Her oily heart went cold and lurched too hard. She faltered, brought her hands into her bosom, looked around the street accusingly, as if such pain must have been wished on her from someone nearby, and, as her eyes settled on her watching son and her body settled on the asphalt in front of him, she died.

I will not patronize you with my interpretation of this little anecdote. We have outsmarted our lives too much as it is. Understanding is overrated. To hell with it. Yet I will again ask you to consider the depth and scope of your fatherly sacrifices with regard to Ben. I will ask you to do some real thinking for a change. I will ask for these things from you, and I will wait by my window, in my room, in the field—all the while conducting my experiments in silence and the final shedding of my feelings—I will wait for some sign from you that you have heard and are ready to comply, to participate, to finally fulfill your real role as a father to Ben, to ascend, however much it will harm your physical self. I will ask you to do these things. Then I will no longer ask you.

We must always be prepared to admit when a theory is merely lyrical, but fucked in practice. Today it is clear to all of us that the Black Room and the Wind Quota were fine ideas when we first blueprinted Ben's development narrative—in those days when having a child was like writing about something that hadn't happened yet—but now we must concede that Ben does not even resist his daily wind-ambush baths down at the learning pond. He simply allows himself to blow wherever the machine fans carry him, and I suspect that any benefits of this disruption—the technical elements of surviving a weather ambush, for instance—are lost on him. He knowingly walks into the collision every day, having learned nothing, apparently, from the successive regulated wind attacks we designed to occur like an invisible sunset, one made of air, which, according to you, took you and knocked you down and reset you for the next day, breathless and hungry for something new to happen.

It's as though he walks into the same dark alley night after night, even though he knows a man with a knife awaits him. Possibly Ben subscribes to a statistic that asserts perfectly awful events cannot recur with such precision day after day. He cannot believe that a calamity can repeat from the same coordinates, as though every house and every yard and every father can only produce one disaster, and the disaster, once discharged, cannot return to where it was stored. He is not learning from his injuries. It's the old French idea that Father never strikes twice. I forget who said it, but it's a pretty notion, if only it were true. It certainly isn't true about his father.

Let's have some evidence: If you look at Ben's films, particularly the behavior footage of the wind ambush, you'll see that Ben is just a boy who apparently believes that every morning he will be swept from his feet by the wind and slammed into the barn or the silo or the now-crumbling lip of the well, after which he must brush himself off and be on his way, limping and possibly bleeding, but grinning, as if to deny his attackers the pleasure of seeing his pain (although the grin has never been proven to be anything more than acute facial discomfort, a gestural insecurity that the face adopts when other gestures are not forthcoming).

Aside from simply wishing Ben were smarter (which only means I would like to feel more intimidated, surprised, or baffled by him), one must observe that he certainly is no more kite-like or nimble in the wind than he ever was, if such a talent is even possible or useful or interesting, or even a talent at all.

In the end, Ben has fewer maneuvers than a stone. Your idea of a "Kite Boy" was once provocative, in the perfectly harmless way that ideas are: potent and fascinating and useless. To be fair, there was a time when we all wanted to envision Ben somehow immune to what made the rest of us so "miserable," before we understood how sadness was dosed over our household in a systematic, midwestern, medicinal wind, emotions carried in on the unstoppable weather: a relentless blowing, blowing, blowing, wherever we went, a skin-piercing wind that made the inside of our bodies so distractingly loud and cold and raw, no matter what clothes we wore and what walls we erected in the field to block it, despite the calisthenics we devised to alter how our bodies met or skirted the air. Before we windproofed our lives with special birds and thick trees and houses built just so, when even deep in our beds there was this inevitable final voiding of privacy, from a nature that was so jealous of the objects inside it that it could do nothing but eavesdrop all the time, sending wind on reconnaissance inside every porous body to snoop around, dispatching the air as a final spy to ensure that absolutely nothing, nothing, nothing would occur without its notice.

It was thus easy to dream of fashioning a boy who would evolve beyond this vulnerability to such meddling, hard air.

An immunity we longed for, if not for ourselves, then for our little person. He would be shielded. What else was evolution for but to correct the deepest miseries of a person, and shouldn't Person Rearing in America simply accelerate our mastery over the Sorrows from the Outside, so that people might live in secret, be less noticed, more covert, possibly untraceable? Did God not ask Jesus to be new and unknown, to crawl through water, to move his hands in front of his enemies' mouths so their language would be rendered babble? Did Jesus not stitch his own mouth after filling it with cloth, rendering his sermon muffled and anguished? Did not this cloth, and others like it, soaked in the oldest language, become holy, so we could swab ourselves with his word, wash our heads in sermon?

Maybe. Maybe. Maybe. But Ben is simply going to be killed, and this is not an interesting-enough way to die.

When he emerges each Tuesday from the Black Room, it seems that not only speech but also written language alarm him and cause his chest to become flushed, welts blooming on his body as though he were boiling on the inside, his skin poured over him as if it were glue, to hide the real person inside. You'll say that it is the women's speech his body is rejecting, that he has developed a listener's rash to the mouth allergens spewed out when we open up our heads to speak. Go ahead and say it. I know your argument by heart. I know you by heart. The things you say are just symptoms of your corrupted mouth, your distorted palate. But each Tuesday evening, Ben is submitted to my Motherhood Messages, on cassette tape, at ample volume. And although we can't judge by his emotions, which I understand to be decoys meant to put me off my guard and compel me to repeat the mistakes of Persons That Have Died™, who once indulged in The Having of Emotions, and thus digressed their entire lives into indulgent and self-congratulatory reflection, pursuing Rewards of Insight and Rewards of the Mouth, I have observed Ben to soften at his own mouth as he curls his pajama-clad body around the tape machine in the Affection Room. His breathing goes slow, and his lips become moist and slack before he falls asleep.

The small wet mouth is an interesting symptom in child rearing. When it is exhibited, it is the only time I am almost tempted to touch him. I avoid the booth at such times. I wring my cloth until the feeling passes. I do my stretches. Possibly a bit of duct tape over the area would discourage my impulse. Yet that would clog his language apparatus, and it is on Ben's language apparatus that we are pinning most of our hope, looking for unprecedented utterances. New words, old words said newly, nonwords, sounds. Maybe something else. It's a big hole there. Anything could come out of it.

Hear me out. If we are to have a person between us, we should have a full-sized one with a fully functioning mouth, an enlarged and intricately structured palate, a cavity that will *accommodate* as well as *generate* the messages that will command the citizens of the town and elsewhere. We require a boy who will come to use the Ohio language like the other alleged children in the neighborhood (I absolutely refuse to comment, but every word in that entire phrase should be in quotes, italicized, underlined, asterisked, and, if that fails to send up a warning flag, fucking burnt to the ground). Even if the things Ben comes to say do not subscribe to our traditions of sense, even if he turns out to be a shouter and complainer.

Or, or, or. Using words in other popular ways, as we have observed from him all too many times:

- Breaking open his own mouth with foreign languages (the Ambassador).
- Redescribing basic household events in terms of his own discomfort (the Patient).
- Bemoaning his exclusion from events that occurred before he was born or while he was asleep or otherwise incapacitated (the Anachronist)
- Remarking on conditions and situations already observed by others (the Fact Checker).
- Speaking in an accent, to deflect attention from his real voice (the Traveler).
- Remarking on his own feelings, presuming outside interest in the statistics of his inner life (the Teacher).
- Using words of encouragement and approval when others make observations, because he chooses to be viewed as an enabler and an approver (the Mother).
- Asking questions of others merely to hint at the questions he wishes were asked of him (the Poet).
- Describing activities he plans one day to undertake in order to suggest an attractive version of himself that has yet to occur (the Scheduler).
- Mentioning information he has read about (the Stringer).
- Commenting with value phrases on the various things that can be seen or heard or felt, positing himself as a prioritizer or cataloger of whatever can be perceived (the Goalie).
- Or finally a young man who only uses language to condemn his parents for launching him in the first place,

accessing the blame region of language and utilizing it fully to discredit us (the Person).

It should not matter to us what strategies Ben concocts as a young language user in America, nor should his father and mother compete to apprentice him to their own separate approaches, weak and useless as they are: using words to articulate accomplishments or reasons to be loved (father), using words to describe one's own shortcomings so fluently that pity is invoked (mother, long ago), using words to lull employees into slavish compliance (father), or no longer using words at all, unless quietly typed to her former husband in a final missive (mother).

Regardless of how we each have failed to traffic in language with any newness at all, a failure we can mourn at some other time (though I would suspect even our mourning style to be derivative, repetitive, selfish), let us for now please agree not to launch an undernourished boy who will be broken open one day and left to fail this world forever on one of our doorsteps (not that your quarters feature a doorstep, though your current home is certainly nicer than where you're going). For my part, I should not like to feel responsible for a dead boy, particularly as I near completion of my Responsibility Fasting Procedure, my Obligation Shedding Schedule. A decease at this time, particularly of my own child, would be a clear setback, would implicate me in feelings I am no longer interested, or lazy enough, to have.

Because of this speech allergy, Jane Dark is no longer able to read to him from *The Unwritten Books of Susan* without Ben turning rigid and blank. Can language of this sort act directly on his spine? I know that you advocate a children's rash, or at least that you have seen rashes as a sign of change, the body fighting the world, for if it is not in collision, then it must be in retreat, and thus weak and afraid, doomed. "What is a rash?" you asked me once while we huddled in the back of a Dating Shelter in Akron, seeking our own private water fountain. Before I could shed my assumptions, as I had learned to do, and formulate some new and impressively lateral idea about skin inflammation as it relates to anxiety, ambition, and behavior concealment—because back then I suffered from a panic to produce for you ideas that were just beyond comprehension, odd and inscrutable enough to baffle or intimidate my audience—you spoke rapidly about armor and inner wind, the body's topography, how people map one another and produce personality landscapes on their skin, so that the flesh is a mirror, and the rash only reflects the disease of the person nearby, a theory positing the skin as a truth serum, what you called "the divining layer," "more revealing than a fossil" (your words), which, even if true, does not justify a collection of pelts in the home, or the encouragement of intact skin shedding in a certain man's daughter.

Let's say, for the sake of being extremely bored of this argument of yours, and to demonstrate my indifference to it, my "supremacy" (your words), my ability to concede to ideas I privately know to be romantic and flawed, that Ben's rash is a sign that I am ill, or that we women here are wrong in the body and soon to decline, and Ben is reflecting our decay by adopting raised red bumps all over his chest. My son is a flag for my disorder. We have children so they might advertise our inadequacies. Giving birth is akin to producing *proof*. The very existence of Ben proves something; his body is litmus, an Empathy Skin. Let's say it. Consider it said. It has been said.

Now, here on the women's side of the house we are left with a boy who would scratch his chest until it bled if we didn't glove his hands, and I must fall back on what I'm sure you'll determine a conservative notion: that Ben should not gouge at his chest so ruthlessly. If he is to dig, he should dig away from his body. That is what backyards are for: to dig holes, to maybe dig holes big enough for people, to then put people in the holes, and cover them back up again with dirt. To then recite statements atop these holes pertaining to the people within them, to describe atop these holes those people in the holes. To praise them, salute them, send them faithfully away. No hole in Ben's chest will be big enough to hold another person. There are no graves located on people's bodies. We do not exhume our own chests for other people's bones. Digs do not occur at these sites. We do not plant stones there to mark the fallen. We do not place flowers. The body is not a hole, not a grave. Ben should not dig there. My justification? His chest covers his heart. Or perhaps you'd like to downplay the importance of the heart, as well.

Now, final topic. You and I. What is left for us? We will not fuck again. We will not meet. We will not touch each other, or converse. You will not see me again. I will see images of you: photographs, drawings, acetate motion charts. Possibly some EKG readings. A short film will be made of your departure.

Which leaves, finally, Ben's future.

If Ben elects voluntary paralysis when he turns eighteen, and inhabits a silent suit down at the Akron Stillness Center, I would at least like him to have experienced, for the purposes of later dismissal, the dubious pleasures and vague disappointments of running, jumping, sliding, and walking, the dullness and fascination of being able to lead his own body off road into the woods, up ladders, onto roofs, or down the emotion-reduction luge chute, not least because these technologies of personal transport might deliver him beyond the compound of the house and its satellite buildings—its barns and silos and fainting tanks—into the city, and to the natural preserves he has probably noticed pulsing somewhat dimly on the horizon.

He spends enough time on the roof for me to guess that he is one of those young people interested in the distance, in objects that he can see but cannot touch. Since you and I discovered in our time together that touching something, such as a boy, or each other, infected it with ourselves and thus spoiled our curiosity for it, because our attractions for others were based on our repulsion for ourselves, it will probably be useful to allow Ben access to those regions we most wish him to dismiss (other people, other places), to let him realize on his own how dull the world can be. Let us not imprison him before giving him a chance to imprison himself.

I do not share Ben's interest in the distance, and I do not want to presume to know the boy (I am not interested in the trap of empathy or the *false comfort* |any other kind?| of understanding), but he must be looking at something.

Thinking back on my own life, which technically does not interest me, there was a time when I felt a distracting curiosity about mountains, as much as I tried to discipline myself against it. Something felt unfinished in me when I regarded the hills and swells around my childhood home, areas my father referred to as "mistakes in the terrain." I thought, Even though the world spins so fast, how come it hasn't smoothed down these so-called mountains? Why are they still so lumpy when the wind has leveled everything else? Are mountains just a failure of wind? Shouldn't the earth be less interesting? Otherwise what does one *do* with something that is merely pretty? And ultimately: Why am I being tested this way? I felt as though I had eaten someone else's emotions and they were swimming in my body, that I had strong feelings that weren't my own. I was hosting another person inside myself, like that man in the famous book who eats his family to protect them from the sun. My choice: either digest the person or perform it out of myself, invert myself and cleanse my feelings. (This is what it is to feel things: to feel like someone else.) It wasn't the loss of control that made me sick, but my utter unfamiliarity with myself, the disappointment of discovering reactions and attitudes to the world that seemed so highly predictable. Here I was, just another girl responding to beauty, and the inevitability of this disposition to the world seemed like a terrible loss of control, a vastly disappointing conformity I had hoped to be exempt from.

What did I do? I took my father's advice: "Go away." I overcame the problem by wearing a modified falcon's hood, what my mother called my "visor," which defeated my attempts to discern the horizon and reminded me that if an object was out of my reach, it most likely belonged to someone else, and of course, as I believe, affection should not occur without possession.

A phrase worth repeating.

Certainly we can agree that the boy should see more and that he should gain these visions by his own power, by zooming in on objects through his own effort, running toward trees, other people, and so forth. Yet you'll understand that no one on the women's side of the house is inclined to drive Ben to these scenes, even if the lake and the so-called trees are supposedly "wonderful," as you repeatedly used to tell me during that time when you believed that sharing your opinion with me would make me care for you more, or implicate me permanently in your ideas and life, as though learning something of your bias was actually going to prove useful to either of us. By sharing interpretations of a world that refused to accommodate our ideas, we only embarrassed each other and dramatized our own ignorance. An injunction of silence in our relationship would have quite possibly forestalled our disappointing discoveries about each other. Your words: "To know someone is to know why you should leave them."

The women's use of cars, *as I'm sure you know,* has been attended by collision, ambush, and pistol fire, and we are not prepared to lose any more women or equipment to those excursions when we have everything we need right here, including enemies we can at least see. Please note that this is not an accusation of you or your staff. An accusation would sound more like this:

I'm sure it's a coincidence that every time a female staffer leaves the compound she dies before nightfall, at which point the men's camp lights a celebration fire and sings until dawn.

But even that sounds mild, more like sarcastic innuendo. How about:

Because you had decreasing access to the physical territory we will refer to as "me" (though the naming of my person is a complicated and highly contested endeavor, and I imagine your exhaustion would exempt you from such a difficult task), a place you felt you formerly visited regularly and with my permission, though indeed I only ever allowed passive access, and you then received notice, in the form of silence, that this trespass of yours would never occur again, you took the liberty of canceling what women of mine entered your purview, a cancellation you accomplished with weaponry and subterfuge, with traps you dug in the soil or laced into trees.

But I harp on. The point of all this: Why not take Ben on an outing? Father and son go to the hills. Michael and Ben take a trip in a car. Boy and man eat sandwiches in a box. Colorful napkins. Bring a ball and a bat, your mitts. Take hats, jackets, Ben's sweater. Drive along the road. Enjoy yourselves. Let him see what he sees (extremely important parenthetical remark: you will be watched, you will be watched, you will be watched). And you, by all means, take a good look around while out in the open air with your own little Ben. Take note of the world and its things. Practice remembering the lake and the field and the hills bubbled up in the distance, trees leaning like broken cages over you, the so-called birds asserting their airborne geometry. Take very special note of these sites.

Why? Here is your future in writing: You and I are operating within an inevitability that I have designed. I am proud to announce authorship of the next things that will happen to you. It is best that you learn about them now. A container is being prepared for you: It will contain your body and be possessed of enough dimension for you to spin in place or lie prone, twist on the floor, or crawl several strokes, a repertoire of actions I predict you will soon abandon, though they are among your favorite things to do. One: No one will watch you.

Two: These actions will prove distinctly uncomfortable. Three: It will be impossible for you to cultivate a sense of accomplishment. This is a fancy way to say we are interring you in an underground cell, sending you under, putting you away. Your potential physical velocity will be modest at best, since walls will prevent your acceleration, and collisions lack the complexity of sensation I know that you favor in your experiences. I cannot imagine you throwing yourself against a wall for very long without becoming bored or hurt beyond repair. The container's location is irrelevant, at least to you, since you will be inside of it and lose sense of all other places. But you can be assured that it will be in no such place for persons out walking, or some such other incorrect form of "engaging the day or night" (your words), to come upon you by chance, to hear your shouts, to dig you out and save you and end your *terrible ordeal* (any other kind?).

Sentences of words are being composed at this very moment that will disturb you to hear. They will comprise the entire media of your days and nights in the container, unless darkness counts as a medium, or your own breath counts as a medium, or your own shouts of greeting or strife to persons who are not present or do not actually exist can come to count as a medium, as any distortion of silence is ultimately the attempt of a creature to gain attention, although silence itself is God's medium, as you pointed out, in which case you will enjoy his solo performance of silence for a long, long time. You will be in audience to his expertly crafted silence, his "original nothingness of sound" (your words). His silence will be made and experienced and enjoyed by you alone. Alone, alone, alone.

Is that it? That is not it. Should you care to know, an aperture will be in place in the area commonly known as the ceiling. We will call this the "aperture of contact," and it will be through here that you will be given access to the language we have designed. It will not admit light, this aperture. It will not admit people. It will admit words, but it will not receive them. Think of it as a mouth, though the metaphor ends there. Its larger purpose is for you to guess at, which should give your so-called imagination a small degree of labor, a task that will have to count as your main recreation, since you may require something to do after all, other than to listen to the sentences coming in, so why not be alone there to puzzle with yourself over what exactly is going on?

As such, then, the only choices for you now involve your conduct within the inevitable. Isn't that, after all, where all conduct occurs? And as a former expert of conduct, which you purported to be, and occasionally were, I hope that you will give the matter the very best thoughts you have, and concoct a behavioral endgame that will, at the least, engage those persons required to witness your last moments as a living man. Please be mindful of those of us who must watch you. Give us something to pay attention to.

Will I be there when they lower you into the hole? I will not. Will I toss dirt over the entrance? No. Will I ever visit the hole to speak words there? I cannot answer that; it simplifies my plans. Will I sometimes, at night, go out to the hole and stand there quietly weeping, watching the sun break down over the horizon? No, no, no. I will have no such moments. In fact, I would argue that those are not moments at all. Moments actually *occur*, while these things are crafted with such panic and falsity that they freeze up and in reality do not happen at all—woman weeping over incarcerated man—though they are remembered as if they did. Let's say my body might grace your grave site. I may roll in the soil there. Do I believe in saturating my skin in the soil that covers the man in the chamber? I might. Do I subscribe to blanketing myself in sediment, performing the postures of silence while caked in dirt, exploiting my body as a full-scale listening device modified by the earth that covers a husband? A resonant earth? Do I plan to cultivate and disperse this soil, to distribute it in this and other areas as a muffling tarp, hush crumbs, a layer of silence to finally quiet down the world. Do I?

Knock, knock.

Good-bye,
Jane Marcus

Printed in the United States
by Baker & Taylor Publisher Services